Into the Land of the Clock-Watchers

The Epic Adventures of Prince Ralphie

Into the Land of the Clock-Watchers

The Epic Adventures of Prince Ralphie

Ralphie received his accolade on January 20th 2020,
the Year of the Dragon in the Realm of the Imaginal

Robert Augustus Gerard
&
Georgiana Spadafora

Copyright © 2020
Georgiana Spadafora & Robert Augustus Gerard
All rights reserved.

No part of this book may be reproduced in any form
or by any electronic or mechanical means,
including information storage and retrieval systems,
without prior permission in writing by the copyright owners.
The only exception is by a reviewer,
who may quote short passages in a review.

Cover Illustration: Georgiana Spadafora

Printed in the United States of America

Dedication
John Drummer, Jr.

*Words included in the cover illustration
are just a few of Prince Ralphie's favorites from his book of*

The Most Beautiful Words in the World

λόγος *Greek*	*Logos, word, reason, or plan. The divine reason implicit in the cosmos, ordering it and giving it form and meaning.*
Rhapsode *English*	*A person who recites epic poems, especially one of a group in ancient Greece whose profession it was to recite the Homeric poems from memory.*
εὔνοια *Greek*	*A well mind or beautiful thinking—biblical favor. In rhetoric, the goodwill a speaker cultivates between himself and his audience, a condition of receptivity. It is also a rarely used medical term referring to a state of normal mental health.*
Nefelibata *Portuguese*	*A cloud walker. An individual who lives in the clouds of their own imagination or dreams. Someone who doesn't abide by the rules of society, literature, or art.*
μεράκι *Greek*	*Doing something with soul, creativity, passion or love—when you put "something of yourself" into what you're doing, whatever it may be.*

continued

continued

Dânesh *Persian*	*Literally translates to wisdom, knowledge, and science.*
ἀρετή *Greek*	*Excellence of any kind, moral virtue. In its earliest appearance this notion of excellence was ultimately bound up with the notion of the fulfillment of purpose or function—the act of living up to one's full potential.*
Yūgen *Japanese*	*An awareness of the universe that triggers emotional responses too deep and mysterious for words.*
ψυχή *Greek*	*The breath, the soul, the vital breath, breath of life, the human soul. The soul as the seat of affections and will, the self, a human person, an individual. In Hebrew, a soul, living being, life, self, person, desire, passion, appetite, emotion.*
Ezüsthíd *Hungarian*	*The silvery reflection of the moon in the water. Literally means silver bridge.*
όνειρο *Greek*	*Dream, dreaminess, dreamlike, dreamland. To see, hear, or feel something in a dream—imaginary events seen while sleeping. (Also: óneiro)*

Table of Contents

		Page
Preface		1
Prologue: An Extraordinary Case of Dragonie Wanderlust		3
Chapter		
1	The Wind Whispers in Ralphie's Ears	13
2	Of Peach Trees and Clock Towers	25
3	In Search of Father Time	55
4	And Trouble Ensues	73
5	Into the Land Beyond the Reach of Time	99
6	Returning to the Land of the Clock-Watchers	113
7	The Back Porch Investiture Ceremony	133
The Auparavent: What Came Before		153

Preface

All of what you are about to read in these epic adventures came to pass because, by his mother's stories and chivalric instruction, Ralphie had come to believe that to revive his heraldic ancestral glory all that was necessary for him to do was to go questing, and then record in his journal the more ennobling and emboldening aspects of his experiences.

He believed that these stories, along with a few grand speeches explaining how the stories were connected to each other in his epic search for the Holy Grail, would become the legends he could use to bring back his father's lost kingdom. Thus, by sharing the wisdom of his adventures, he could organically create the foundational myths for a viable, fertile, philosophical kingdom—with its own Round Table!

All this would be accomplished by way of following the Chivalric Code, the Code of the Order of the Heart, and a few other miscellaneous pledges, non sequitur declarations, and sometimes seemingly silly affirmations, just like in the stories of all the other kings and queens he and his mother had read about. Through her careful and patient tutoring she helped him understand the filial duties of a virtuous Green Dragon with a royal lineage.

Later, when he found himself face-to-face with troubling troubles and she wasn't there to guide him, he could close his eyes and hear her gently coaching him, "Read, read, read … then go out and do the right thing!"

Prologue

An Extraordinary Case of Dragonie Wanderlust

Once upon a time, in a modest but comfortable cave, on the outskirts of the dragon village of Ioville, in an enchanted forest, in the Kingdom of the Dragons of the Verbose, in the Land of the Clock-Watchers, there lived a young, unassuming, Green Dragon named Ralphie. To all outward appearances, he was just a plain, ordinary, mild-mannered little dragon, old enough to believe he could conquer the world, but not yet old enough to know how to go about it properly.

Even though Ralphie did his best to be modest and unassuming while he was at school—to fit in with the other dragons—as time went by it became more and more evident to him that he was indeed different from the other dragons in his village. He had surmised that what was different about him was that his imagination could often run away with him, carrying him off to dizzying heights of wonder, by way of wild adventures, that even his closest friends couldn't follow along on; due mainly to his elaborate and convoluted sense of time and place, as well as his often reckless courting of danger. Ralphie comforted himself by telling himself it was the kind of imagination it would take to conquer and rule a kingdom turned upside down by his half uncle and his minions.

He even told his friends that he'd ventured several times alone into the Land of the Clock-Watchers, and that when he'd tried to talk to the adults, they hardly noticed him, because most of them were so busy going here and there that they never looked up to see what was right in front of them! But the children could see him, and they loved to play with dragons! He also told his friends that he'd found that he could walk among the adults almost invisibly, and that he'd visited there often to play with the children. When his friends challenged him on the veracity of his claims, he double-dared them to come along next time—and see for themselves!

Ralphie had no father to guide his footfalls. At times, this made him quite melancholy, especially when he watched the other dragons with their fathers. All he had to hang his hopes on was the saga of a philosopher prince who'd been cut down in the full bloom of his life, a father who would have been king, if things had gone differently in the defining battle of his life. While his mother, he knew, did what she could in place of his father's instruction to embolden him and give him an ennobling legacy to live up to, somehow it never seemed to quench his youthful yearnings; his ambitions to make his own arrival on the stage of history and reclaim his family's birthright.

♦♦♦♦♦

The forest Ralphie lived in was at the narrow end of a great canyon, with the village itself situated at the crossroads below the cave-homes of the dragons, which all had breathtaking views of the lush pine forest below. The rock walls in that end of the canyon were full of caves, like a great Swiss cheese. Some of these caves were even interconnected, which lent them to cheese storage, as well as wine storage, and salt storage, and, of course, gold storage. So that most of the dragons in his village were employed, in one fashion or another, in the storage business. At the crossroads there were a few stores offering groceries and hardware and dragon whatnots, and there was even a blacksmith. There was also a café, and a library, and even an outdoor theatre for plays.

The cave Ralphie and his mother lived in had a narrow opening, off an immense terrace landing, beyond which it gave way to a cozy home with private chambers for their sleeping rooms, and of course, some storage. Past the entry, in the main chamber, the stone floor was carpeted with oriental rugs, and there were comfortable, overstuffed chairs, placed invitingly in small groups around the room. On the walls were hung old family coats of arms, along with swords, and spears, and woolen tapestries displaying long past days of glory, as well as portraits of favored ancestors. And somehow, due to a hidden crack high in the domed ceiling, light was reflected inside, so that it wasn't ever dank or dark, but rather airy, and felt open, and yet the rain never got in.

The overall ambience of the main room was that of the interior of a medieval grand hall, just on a much smaller scale. It included a living area, as well as a kitchen with an immense fireplace that a grown dragon could stand upright in, and a family-dining area as well, with a round table surrounded by four well-worn leather wingchairs, and books piled high throughout, on shelves and tables, and even on the floor. But the most extraordinary feature of their home, a feature shared by each home in that village, was the spectacular view of the entire valley they had. And by just rolling a big rock away from one wall of the front room, they could see the sweep of the forest below, for miles around.

◆◆◆◆◆

Thus, the setting and sweep of his circumstance naturally lent itself to innumerable inspirations for bold and vital adventuring. For which, at least to Ralphie's way of thinking, a grand name was required.

Consequently, one evening when his mother was in the kitchen preparing his favorite dinner of toad toe stew, something they had almost every night, a mulligan stew of a sort, and Ralphie was at the table, sitting sideways in his father's wingback chair with his legs over one arm, kicking the air and his body twisted into the corner of the other arm, the talk turned to how, of all the great names in the world, he had come to be named Ralphie.

He had learned, the hard way, that Ralphie was a name that had done him ill service in life thus far, and he suspected it would be equally clunky at court. And so, because he somehow knew intuitively, in his bones, that it was indeed his destiny to be great, he thought a grander name, a name that would command respect, and announce him even before anyone met him, would be much better.

Thus, in that vein he asked, "Why'd you name me Ralphie? It's not the name I would've picked for a knight with a grand destiny. I would've picked the name Alexander Augustus, or Caesar Augustus! You know, something with Augustus in it, because in Latin it means 'the great'!"

"That's exactly why we chose it, because Ralphie *is* a great name in our family!" replied his mother, somewhat facetiously. "You were named after your uncle Ralph, the one in the picture in your room. He died heroically in one of the many Great Wars on Ignorance our family has fought in over the centuries. And *he* was named after a hundred generations of legendary Ralphie's before him—that's what makes it a great name!"

His mother often liked to add some spice to her stories to keep his attention, giving them more flavor by making them more fantastical. And she did so now. So, without waiting for him to object on spurious grounds, she added a casual but crucial detail to his namesakes' legends. "Have I ever told you before that the Ralphie in the picture in your room was named after *his* uncle? And that his uncle was the pirate who designed the pirate flag with the skull and cross bones! He made it that way to scare the enemy before the fight, so they'd just give up and runaway out of fright."

Ralphie's ears tingled at the mere mention of pirates, his other favorite subject of research when he wasn't studying knight errantry. It also bolstered his uncle's derring-do image for him, because pirating involved a lot of swashbuckling. So he asked, "Really? He did? What ship did he captain?"

"I think it was … the Fiery Dragon? Or was it the Happy Adventure?" she replied thoughtfully, tapping her lips with her claw. "I forget right now," she remarked. "But it doesn't matter. The point is he was great because he was really a peace-loving dragon at heart and would rather avoid fighting whenever possible. Some pirates, like your uncle's uncle, would rather frighten you than fight you. Some pirates can be very clever, you know. They like to bluff and beguile, and even bamboozle people, just to avoid hurting them. But that's another story," she added mysteriously.

Even though disappointed at not hearing the full tale, Ralphie felt heroicized by the association nonetheless. "So you mean I'm part pirate too?" he puffed out enthusiastically.

"Yes! Yes, you are," she laughed. "Except he was a distant uncle, and that's a wild branch of the family, so you're mostly philosopher prince. At any rate, we knew it to be an honorable namesake—as family heraldic traditions go—all your uncle Ralphie's being peace loving, good-natured Green Dragons, fighting on the right side of history like they did, and that's why we chose it to be your christening name."

From that night forward, Ralphie knew his ancestral name was indeed hallowed, and so would announce himself at the dinner table each night as "Sir Ralphie Augustus"—Ralphie the Great—decked out in a magician's cap that he'd won on the midway when a traveling theatre troupe had come to town, which could be folded into several different shapes, to be used for theatrical disguises, along with a pair of trousers his mother had sewn for him that had a special opening for his tail and extra space in the haunches. As well as the topcoat of a secondhand band uniform and a gray blanket that he'd fashioned into a cape, and clasped together with a clothespin. This costume was further enhanced with whatever else was close at hand on the table that he could use to make his point, be it a loose utensil, a platter of fruit, or a common goblet.

♦♦♦♦♦

Thus, with that kind of royal and ennobling ancestry, and given his natural imaginal agency, Ralphie knew it wouldn't do for the prince of such a rich inheritance to sit at home on the landing and just watch the world go by.

So each night, after his mother had read him still one more adventure story to spur on his dreams, he would sleepily mumble, just as he'd done a thousand nights before, "Tomorrow, Mama ... tomorrow I'm going questing ... to find the Holy Grail ... and then ... and then I'm going to reclaim our kingdom ... and build you a new castle ... with a moat ... so you'll be safe ... and a grand hall for extravaganzas ... and a tall tower for surveying our lands ... and ..."

"When you're ready, Ralphie, when you're ready," she'd whisper lovingly, stroking his cheek, before kissing him goodnight and softly closing his bedroom door.

Then one fine day, it actually happened! Ralphie set out, almost absentmindedly, caught up in his imaginary world as usual, to explore as much as he could of the world beyond his home. Because he believed it *was* his natural inheritance, his birthright as a freethinking, incurably curious dragon to go forth and quest, to go adventuring … to ennoble and embolden himself … so that he'd be properly ready when the moment of truth arrived and he came face-to-face with the usurpers and the Bronze Dragons, in a do-or-die battle for his rightful place among the defenders of the Chivalric Code!

Chapter 1

The Wind Whispers in Ralphie's Ears

So it was that on one sunny day, when the sun was bathing the world in warmth, and in the fields the grain was dancing to the music of the winds, and the world was at rest, and it looked like nothing was really happening, it so happened that the wind whispered in Ralphie's ears that the road was inviting him to cross the hills and adventure into the distance to see what lay beyond his village.

Thus it was that on an ordinary day, like any other day, the adventure of his lifetime began, and he set forth from his home into the world that was his kingdom to claim. But he had no army, no ministers, no bureaucracy, no court, no nothing, except his imagination to conquer its vast territories. Nevertheless, he packed a hobo's bindle and set out.

In the bindle, he packed his treasured old dictionary, his reading glasses, a candle in case he found himself cornered in a dark place, a rusty Swiss Army knife with only one blade that opened, the spork, a picture of his parents that he kept in a locket, as well as sundry other items he thought might come in handy in tight situations.

When the actual adventure started, Ralphie found himself at the top of one of the distant hills near his home, absentmindedly walking down a road that led to a village in a faraway valley. From his perch on the top of the hill, he could see the entire village, white-walled and red-roofed, gleaming in the afternoon sun, laid out in the middle of the cultivated green fields around it. Just beside the village, running along one side of it, he could see a silvery river that snaked its way through the valley.

Near the river, Ralphie saw several Clock-Watcher children who looked to be about his age and size, playing and swimming. He could hear their laughter and feel their high spirits, and it made him want to join in too. So he made his way toward them. But as he got closer he hesitated and decided to hide behind some bushes near the riverbank, because they were strangers to him, and so he couldn't help wondering, *What if they're not friendly princes like me? What if this is their kingdom? I could be trespassing!* But then, as he was about to return to the road, one of the girls, and then one of the boys, caught sight of him in the underbrush.

"Hi! I'm Georgiana. Who're you?" the girl who'd spotted him sang out in a friendly way.

Cautiously, he came out from behind the bushes, his bindle and stick still on his shoulder, and said, "I'm Ralphie." He left off the Augustus part of his name because he wasn't feeling so great right then.

"Where'd you come from?" asked the boy, apparently unmoved by Ralphie's dragonieness.

"I come from …" he started to say, then hesitated again. Because, for the life of him, he couldn't rightly explain where he came from, geographically speaking, as he'd just wandered off. So he answered somewhat evasively, "I come from the Kingdom of the Dragons of the Verbose. My father's king of all the loquacious dragons in the land, and my mother, the queen! She can cook up magic spells of all kinds!" Ralphie smiled as he said it, because he thought this double claim of linguistic royalty might impress them. And he knew he could clear up any misunderstandings later, in endless casual conversations.

"Well, all I can say is you certainly don't look like a prince to me!" insisted Georgiana in a nonplussed manner.

This was frustrating to Ralphie. Up until then it'd been a pretty good day, and he didn't want to have to prove anything to anyone without good cause, no matter how smart she thought she was. *She could just be a smarty-pants type of person*, he thought to himself.

Nonetheless, even though he was aware that he was being a touch braggadocious, he continued riskily, he just couldn't help himself, "I'm a legacy prince of all the great peripatetic philosopher kings of all time!" He hoped she would not know such big words and high-flying ideas, and therefore stop being so impish.

"What kind of prince is a 'peri-pathetic' prince?" Georgiana asked the boy next to her.

Ralphie immediately corrected her. Again, he just couldn't help himself. "The word is peripatetic, not peri-pathetic!" he said, satisfied that he'd outsmarted a smarty-pants, as he rummaged in his bindle for his dictionary, opening it to the *P's*, and then to the word *parry*, as in sword fighting, because he'd underlined it, then on to peripatetic, which he'd also underlined. "See … see here," he announced triumphantly, stabbing at the word with his claw, "it means my kingdom is everywhere I choose to walk!"

He was glad he'd packed his dictionary, even though it was heavier than all the other items in his bindle, because you never knew when you might need a good, big, solid word to knock some dimwitted ogre or smarty-pants person in the head with; figuratively for the latter, and for real with the former!

Georgiana, still unimpressed and incredulous, turned to the boy in confusion with a shrug of her shoulders.

The boy looked back at her, shrugged his shoulders too, and snickering, stated, "Oh, that just means he's a bindle stiff!" Which made them both giggle.

"No I'm not!" Ralphie countered indignantly. "Anyway, my kingdom's a different kind of kingdom than a regular kingdom—it's a philosophical kingdom!" he added, trying to clarify the matter.

"Well, what makes you think you're not in *our* kingdom?" she argued, while her friend nodded his agreement.

"Because it's not like that!" Ralphie protested. "My kingdom's an invisible, imaginal kingdom of chivalric ideas. It's a philosophical kingdom … created by people like you … and dragons like me—a kingdom of our own making!"

He was very pleased with this description. So pleased in fact, that as he pondered the wondrousness of the words he'd just spoken, he began to see his kingdom unfold before all of them, and in that moment he realized that he was talking about King Arthur's Round Table kingdom, and how the best thing about King Arthur's Round Table was that everyone was equal. And so he couldn't help blurting out, "And the best thing about it is that I'm not your subject … and you're not mine! We're all in the same kingdom, philosophically speaking."

"Well, I still say you don't look like any prince I ever knew! Where's your crown? Where's your scepter?" Georgiana insisted, still skeptical.

Ralphie began to see that trying to explain everything about his philosophical kingdom would take too long, so he just let the remark pass. After all, he just wanted to play. Luckily for him, they too just wanted to play and didn't ask any more tricky questions, and because by now all the other children, having seen Ralphie as well, had stopped playing their games of hoops, and marbles, and of course stilt-walking, and had drawn near with great excitement and curiosity.

To say they were all rosy-cheeked and bright-eyed, would too generously describe them. As Ralphie stared into their mud-smeared faces, he thought they almost looked like a peasant army awaiting instruction, or maybe a gang of highwaymen awaiting instruction, or maybe usurpers awaiting instruction. Regardless, to him they looked like a motley crew that needed instruction. Most wore ill-fitting clothes, and looked like they hadn't bathed in a week. Some had gap-toothed smiles, having lost their baby teeth. While others sported haircuts that looked like their mothers had used dull shears on them. Yet, despite their disheveled and rough appearance, they were all smiling enthusiastically.

"Who are you?" one shouted out.

"Where did you come from?" yelled another.

"What are you doing here?" yet another wanted to know.

"How'd you get here? Did you fly?" and "How high can you fly?" and "How fast?" and "What's the farthest place you ever flew to?" and "Can you fly to the moon?" and "Can you give us rides up into the clouds?" clamored the others, along with a million other questions regarding dragons in general.

In the turbulence of their boisterous enthusiasm, and since he didn't really know them, they were quickly becoming an unruly mob in Ralphie's eyes. And not wanting to become the focus of their attention, simply because he was different, and because he'd heard many stories of dragons who'd crashed and died showing off their flying skills, usually by giving rides, Ralphie knew he had to think fast and somehow distract them from his dragonieness.

"I know! I know!" he exclaimed somewhat shrilly. "We could play the Knights of the Round Table!" This, he could see, caught everyone's attention. So he began giving instruction, explaining the rules of the game and the very important Chivalric Code in a more commanding voice.

As the children listened, they all quickly became swept away with the idea of playing the Round Table game with a dragonie prince who claimed he knew a thing or two about quests and imaginary kingdoms. But then, as he continued his speechifying, they grew restless, and began to look around, spying out potential armaments and flags of royal color and rank.

And before Ralphie could even finish, they all began running about excitedly, gathering sturdy sticks, and pieces of cloth, and abandoned turtle shells, and a dozen other things that were laying about, which they quickly fashioned into capes and veils, and heraldic banners and pennants, and swords and shields and helmets. In a flash, they were all attired in knightly regalia, some with armor that was dirty white and others with armor dark as a moonless night, because each of the children already knew which side he or she wanted to fight on, since they'd played knight errant games before.

But suddenly, they all stopped what they were doing, and stood frozen, staring at Ralphie with big eyes—apparently overawed by the thought of playing one of their favorite games with their newfound dragon friend. So they just stood and looked at him and each other with stupefied faces, but not for long. Then, as if on a silent signal, they set upon one another, before Ralphie had even finished giving his instructions, and as if he hadn't said a word about not ganging up, or showing mercy, or helping the weak and the oppressed.

Ralphie tried his best to regain control, first by clearing his throat loudly, and then by fluttering his wings. Both of which went completely unnoticed. So, in a last futile attempt to get their attention, he tried breathing fire, which just came out as pops and whistles. It seemed the more he tried to take back control, the more hectic things became. The sounds of laughter, and the clatter and clang of sword fighting, and pleas for help and mercy, and shouts of victory and surrender filled the air. The mayhem got so raucous that soon enough Ralphie just gave up and joined in with all the swashbuckling, dying heroically at least seven times that afternoon, until eventually they were all played out, and the sun was about to set.

As the playing wound down, distant dinner bells were heard on the breeze. At which the children began to gather their toys and started heading back to their homes in the village.

Unfortunately for Ralphie, it was too far to go back to his home now, now that the light was fading. So he knew he was going to have to camp by the river that night. He'd camped out of doors with friends and schoolmates before, so he wasn't very much afraid to do it on his own this time. He didn't like the idea of being alone, but he didn't want to go into the village either. The parents of the children who had come to trust him might not be as trusting. They might not appreciate dragons and their wandering ways.

As she was about to leave, Georgiana ran back to where Ralphie was standing. "I still say you don't look like any prince I've ever seen! But I don't care ... I'm glad we're friends!" she exclaimed happily, throwing her arms around him. "Are you going to be here tomorrow?"

"Tomorrow? No, no I'm not—I'm questing! But you could come with me," he offered, hoping she would so he wouldn't be alone.

"Oh, I wish I could," she sighed. "But I can't. "There're chores I've got to do. And the animals won't be happy if they don't get fed," she finished, her words drifting off into silence.

"I understand," was Ralphie's only response, as her explanation seemed pretty definitive to him. So he made no protest and just hugged her back, and waved a final farewell to the other children.

Then, as if he truly had a proper quest to go on, he started off a little way down the trail with great intent. When he thought they couldn't see him, he ducked into the dense foliage by the river and waited until he couldn't see them anymore. Hidden by the many bushes and trees that grew there, Ralphie unfurled his bindle, made a hammock out of the bindle cloth, and strung it between two large oak trees.

He was so tired from all the playing that as soon as he'd made his bed, without making a campfire or even having anything to eat, he got in and curled himself into a tight circle. As he lay there, listening to the soothing, murmuring songs of the river spirits, he began kindling warm thoughts about the adventure he'd had that day, and whatever adventures might come in the next few days. And before long, he felt sleep taking over, and so let himself succumb to the warmth of his thoughts and the gentle sway of the hammock.

Chapter 2

Of Peach Trees and Clock Towers

The next day, the sun rudely woke him up. Ralphie had learned that the sun could be quite annoying when he camped outdoors, the way it prickled him with jabs of light on his eyelids and heated his face until he couldn't ignore it anymore, finally making him get up.

"Good morning, Mr. Sun," he yawned ruefully.

"Ruefully" was another big word Ralphie had underlined recently. It meant "respect without pleasure," as in he didn't take pleasure in being awakened so early, right when his dreams were just about to reveal themselves.

Mr. Sun didn't answer Ralphie directly—he never did. He just shined on annoyingly until Ralphie knew he was going to have to get up and make something of the day in order to enjoy the best part of the day, the sunset, which always seemed sweeter after a long day of hard adventuring!

Mr. Sun was just one of a handful of timekeepers that Ralphie had to deal with each day. And even though he wasn't a clock-watcher himself, he was still mindful of the passing of time. Some of the dragons in his village believed the great Mr. Sun had invented time, and that he was the father of all life on earth. But to Ralphie, these stories of Mr. Sun's possible legendary greatness didn't take away his annoying sting that morning.

Sometimes Ralphie wasn't keen on the great Mr. Sun, and other times he was grateful he came to check on him every day, and sometimes he missed him when it was cloudy and cold. But on this particular day, the day after his epic adventure had begun, it would've been just fine with Ralphie if Mr. Sun had let him sleep in.

Soon after that prickly beginning though, as his stomach growled and rumbled, sounding as if there was a little dragon inside of him, Ralphie forgot about Mr. Sun and started to think about his growling stomach, because he hadn't eaten since the day before.

This need to eat something nutritious and delicious every day was another kind of timekeeper of sorts that also marked the passing of time in terms of how he spent his day. Ralphie's hunger was an irresistible force that couldn't be denied, and demanded his full attention every minute until satiated.

He'd named this demanding feeling of emptiness Mr. Hungry Time, obviously. And when he'd finished eating whatever it was he'd eaten, he'd call it Mr. Happy Time, of course. They were friendly adversaries, not-so-subtle forces that also provoked a sense of the passing day, one of the few markers of time that Ralphie had ever known before his epic adventure into the Land of the Clock-Watchers had begun.

Up until that fateful day, when he'd wandered away from his home in the enchanted forest, Ralphie knew of no other ways of measuring time, nor had any need to. Up until then, he had lived in a world where time had an intuitive sensibility—Hungry Time, Happy Time, Adventure Time, and Dream Time—any of which could happen anytime, day or night.

As he looked around the unfamiliar forest, Ralphie realized he didn't want the children he'd played with the day before to find him still there, where they'd parted. Because then they might guess he'd not gone questing, and therefore might just be a bindle stiff after all. They might then tease him for being a lost soul, and not at all a prince of a far-off kingdom of dragons.

Even though he didn't know where he was going, or what kind of kingdoms he might come across, or who he might meet along the way, Ralphie knew for certain he was going onward into the fantastical future, which he was confident was just downstream a little more. This made him feel brave and possibly recklessly adventurous ... and well, like he was somebody who just might have an adventure or two to pursue beyond his own village!

Right there and then he also decided to christen his questing to be Knight Errantry of the First Order! Which was something he'd read about extensively, but didn't quite know what it meant in practical detail. He just liked the way being a knight errant spoke to his sense of familial birthright. Like it was a life he was destined to live, like his mother had said, full of adventure and grace and chivalric derring-do!

So, after waking up and gathering his belongings back into his bindle, Ralphie embarked on his first official quest. He started up the trail from the river and onto the road. As soon as he got there, he could again see the children of the village playing outside the city wall. Once again he was overcome with a desire to play with them, and despite his many misgivings, he started walking toward them. He just couldn't help himself.

As he got closer, even though he was still quite far away, one of the children and then another and then another, started towards him too. They waved, at which he fluttered his wings in response, just to show off, even though his mother had warned him countless times not to. As he made his way toward them, they all started running excitedly in his direction. He could see that the running had drawn the attention of a tall person, an adult, probably a teacher, with a whistle that dangled from a lanyard around her neck, which she used to call all the children to line up.

She seemed very excited and blew the whistle several times, and was talking to them in shouts he couldn't quite make out because of the distance, but it certainly seemed to him that his presence had frightened her. As he should have known it would, by way of his mother's warnings.

As they lined up, she urged them to hurry, and ushered them through a gate in the wall. They were in so much of a hurry that gloves and balls and bats and hats and coats were left on the field as she closed the gate in the wall with a slam, sealing the children inside.

He knew from experience that very few adults listened to dragons, and he'd seen adults say and do all kinds of strange things whenever dragons were rumored to be in the vicinity. They'd say ugly things about them when they came around, and then gather their kids, and their neighbors' kids, and any loose kids mucking about, and run away and hide behind locked gates and battened doors whenever they sight of one.

That's why Ralphie only played with children; they knew he wasn't someone to be terrified of, that he was in fact just a very friendly Green Dragon. But this reaction, by the adult with the whistle, frightened him as he looked again and now saw several adults peering over the wall, all of them shouting, "Go away!" with various kinds of sticky-words and stone-cold stares.

This happened almost every time Ralphie left his village and ventured into the Land of the Clock-Watchers and approached other children whenever there were adults around, so he'd learned to be careful. He also knew there were many strange and dangerous things that came out of the forest sometimes, and so didn't take their reactions as personal per se, as what they did was done out of an overabundance of caution out of a shared fear of the unknown. Still, he was afraid of what they might do in their terrific fright, and so he ran back into the forest and didn't stop until he got to the river.

From where he stood, Ralphie could see the river was too wide to swim across, and he could also see that the current was too swift, so that even if he did try, he might end up miles downstream. And if he took flight, everyone would notice, and they would raise the town's dragon alarms, and pitchfork mobs might form, and then who knows what might happen! And even though he could out-run or out-fly them, his questing had already begun, and he felt it was his destiny to venture further into the Land of the Clock-Watchers, and not retreat in the face of fear. He was, after all, a knight errant on the adventure of a lifetime! Thus, being left with no other choice, he began to make his way along the riverbank, moving stealthily through the underbrush until he was far away from the village.

As he snaked his way along the river's edge, he would occasionally sneak up the embankment to see if there were any people around. As he moved farther from the village, he could see that there were fewer and fewer, so from time to time he'd sneak into the open and grab a tomato out of a field or an apple out of an orchard.

Around lunchtime, he got lucky and found a couple of duck eggs, and near the river he found a bunch of fragrant mushrooms along with some watercress, and made a kind of an omelet out of it all. Which he cooked by heating up a large flat stone by breathing fire on it, and using his tongue as a spatula to fold the omelet. He'd been camping before.

It was on just such an excursion, on the edge of the forest that ran along the river, that Ralphie spied a peach tree.

It was late in the afternoon by then, and he'd been scavenging all day. Although he wasn't particularly hungry, this one peach, at the end of this one low-hanging branch, seemed to beckon him. In the fading rays of the sun, its fuzz glowed like a halo, and from its stem he could see one drop of nectar had emerged into the sunlight that reflected its ripeness right into his eyes. He was downwind of the tree and could smell the peachy freshness of it too, as if it were calling to him fragrantly—it was a peach made to be eaten by a dragon.

Before he knew what was happening, Ralphie found himself under the tree, reaching for the peach as if it were a sweet gift from Mother Nature herself, as if she were bending the branch low enough to reach his paw. Then, just as he grabbed the juicy fruit, a series of bells clamored for attention from a distance! This didn't startle him, because they were distant, but he became mesmerized by their cadence, and froze stock-still in his grasping.

He stood there on his hind legs, semi-paralyzed in the rapture of their melodic sound, for he didn't know how long. Then he heard yet another sound, a crackling of twigs and a rustle of leaves being trampled. Suddenly, a bark rang out, and out of the corner of his eye, somewhat hidden by the shadow of the ivy growing on the fence, he could see a young girl and her dog had come up behind him.

A floppy hat and a scarf wrapped loosely around her neck hid some of her face, but still he could see that she seemed to be staring at him—not in a frightened or scared manner, just curiously. The dog, after a couple of warning barks, began to sniff the air downwind of Ralphie. He didn't attack or bark again, but rather seemed as curious as she, and slowly moved closer in Ralphie's direction. Ralphie didn't dare move, of course, but the girl just kept staring at him. For so long, in fact, that he couldn't be still any longer.

So in a soft, almost inaudible tone, he said, "I ... I was just checking to see if your peaches were ripe." And then, thinking quite literally on his toes, he continued, "I'm the peach inspector in these parts." He didn't know how that had popped into his head, but he'd said it, and once it was out of his mouth, there was no going back. So he added, "These peaches are now perfect for harvesting!" And, "Carry on."

He thought this clever and had started back into the forest when he heard her excitedly call out, "Ralphie! Ralphie! Wait! Stop! I can't believe it's you! It's me, Georgiana!" as she removed her scarf and hat. Meanwhile, the dog, having followed the conversation mutely, keenly aware of the warmth in her voice, drew closer to Ralphie with his tail wagging wildly.

Ralphie turned slowly, he could barely trust his eyes in the gathering dusk—but it really *was* Georgiana! He couldn't believe his good fortune. First the bountiful lunch, and now meeting his friend from the day before! All of which surely had to mean that he really was on a quest—and the Grail Castle was soon to be found, because serendipity doesn't just happen.

"What're you doing here? And whoever heard of a dragon being a peach inspector? That's just silly!" Georgiana scoffed laughingly, as she made her way closer to Ralphie, carrying a large bushel basket.

"I was just getting a few peaches for …" he said sheepishly and somewhat guiltily without finishing. "But what're *you* doing here?"

"I'm here to pick some peaches for my mother's pies. She sells them at the farmers' market in town. So only the ripest ones will do! Do you want to help me?" Noticing Ralphie glancing nervously at the dog, she added, "Oh, this is my dog, Red. He's my personal bodyguard!" Red, upon hearing his name, wagged his tail even more madly, and drooling a slobbery welcome, came closer to Ralphie. "I know he's big and scary looking, but don't worry, he never hurts my friends."

Being a cautious dragon, Ralphie still hesitated to let his guard down around the dog. For it was well known that Green Dragons were often hunted by hounds, and could be easily caught or trapped when under enchantments or spells, or betrayed by an

Achilles heel revealing itself at the wrong time, or had otherwise become incapacitated in the Land of the Clock-Watchers—and in the duress of the moment, found themselves powerless to use their wings to get away. So he had good reason to be wary.

Seeing his continued uncertainty, as he stiffened and turned a paler shade of green, Georgiana wanted to put him at ease. So she told him reassuringly, "This is my family's farm. There's nothing for you to be scared of here, Ralphie!"

He surveyed Georgiana, then the fence line where she was pointing, following it all the way down the garden path to the back of a house at the end. It was an old farmhouse with a barn next to it, situated on a rise surrounded by rolling hills that had been sectioned off into vineyards and orchards and grain fields, as far as he could see in either direction, and he realized she was telling the truth. In his latest excursion up the bank of the river, he'd evidently come upon a working farm, her family's farm! Now, as he looked closely at the grapes on the grapevines, strung along string lines that extended in rows as far as he could see, ripe and ready for harvest, he saw that some had already been cut, and had been gathered into large baskets in the fields.

Reassured, Ralphie looked at the peach in his paw, then at her, then at Red, then at the basket, and then put his treasure into her basket as a start, and they both smiled. Then, as he took off for the top of the tree, all she could do was gasp in wonder. Although she knew he was a dragon, obviously, in all the games they'd played the day before he hadn't used his wings to really fly, fly. So that when she did see him fly for the first time, she was gobsmacked.

"Oh, Ralphie! Your wings ... your wings are so ... so beautiful! They look ... they look just like hummingbird wings!"

"What do you mean? My wings are *much, much* bigger than a hummingbird's!" he groused indignantly.

"No! Not the size, silly! It's the colors—they're all shimmery, just like a hummingbird's! They're beautiful! Even more beautiful than Pegasus' wings!"

Ralphie blushed and preened at her praise. He'd thought of it before, of course, of being a real-life Pegasus. But in his mind, he was Regasus, the Wonder Dragon! He was often given to fanciful re-namings, in an effort to reimagine his whole world. But those were his private thoughts, and she had seen it on her own, without any coaching, and this made him doubly proud to be who he was.

But there was no time to delay admiring the beauty of his wings in the dimming light, and so he quickly began tossing peaches to her. She soon became so caught up in his larking about, that afterwards she couldn't tell anyone how his wings actually, really, looked; so they said she'd made it all up.

For the next few minutes, he helped her gather the ripest fruit. They made a game of it. He, with his wings in full force, flew to the very topmost branches and then dropped the ripest ones into her basket, as she ran around the tree in circles, catching them.

"Over there, I see more! And look over there, Ralphie! There's even more over there!" calling out her instructions to him on the fly.

Hovering here and there, Ralphie juggled the peaches he'd picked, tossing them to her in threes and fours between doing loop-de-loops and barrel rolls. Georgiana, overwhelmed and weak with laughter from his many antics, almost dropped the basket several times. And while they were gathering their treasure Red danced and barked and ran in circles around her, which made the harvesting an occasion to remember.

By the time the sun had collected its last remaining rays behind the hills on the horizon, they'd gathered enough to fill the basket, which Ralphie calculated was surely enough for several pies! So he imagined that his payment for his extraordinary aerial exploits, in getting the ripest fruits from the top of the tree, was going to be a pie big enough to last him for days! Which made him insanely happy and insanely hungry, all at the same time.

Finally, in the dusky dark, they said their goodbyes to the peach tree.

"Thank you, Polly, for your lovely peaches!" Georgiana called out, dipping into a small curtsy.

"She has a name?" Ralphie asked in surprise, as he picked up the heavy basket to carry it for her.

"Of course! My father let me name her when we planted it. He's the best farmer in the world, you know!" she assured him proudly.

So Ralphie nodded and echoed, "Thank you, Polly Peaches!" and saluted smartly. At which they turned and headed back up the path to the house, with Red proudly leading the way.

At first they talked and laughed loudly, because Ralphie was naturally friendly and funny when he was at ease. But as they got nearer to the house, the conversation quieted, and then fell off completely. Ralphie was feeling guarded again. He began to think that maybe it wasn't such a bright idea to get so close to Clock-Watchers.

Georgiana couldn't help noticing that as they got closer, he was lagging behind more and more. "Don't be afraid," she murmured in a calming voice. "I've already decided you're going to spend the night! There's a safe place for you in the hayloft of our barn."

Ralphie was relieved by this turn of events, as it seemed safer than sleeping outdoors again. But then, just as they came around the barn, the bells he'd heard earlier started again, and he was once again mesmerized. Dropping the basket of peaches, he stopped on the path and stood semi-frozen, ears pointedly at attention, standing on the balls of his feet, straining to get every morsel of sound. He was enraptured.

Just at that moment, the light from the back porch came on, and Red ran straight to the screen door and scratched on it. When it opened, he wiggled his way past and went inside.

Taking advantage of the distraction, Georgiana grabbed Ralphie, pulling him into the barn and all the way up the ladder before he could think to say anything. She did all of this before the bells had quit ringing, and so he stood there in the middle of the loft, in the middle of the hay, still struck dumb, until they'd ceased their clanging. She started kicking the hay in place to make him a bed, which helped bring him out of his haze.

"What was that wondrous sound?" he marveled, trying to hold onto his excitement without giving his insatiable curiosity or limitless ignorance away, remembering what his mother had said about not asking too many questions and becoming annoying.

"That's the clock tower in the square, silly! Haven't you ever heard a clock tower before?"

"A clock tower? What's a clock tower?"

"What do you mean 'what's a clock tower'? Are you telling me you've never heard of a clock tower before?"

"No, never! Where I come from there aren't any clocks, because we have no Clock-Watchers. So what'd be the point of having a clock tower? Whatever it is."

"I've never heard of such a ridiculous thing!" she exclaimed, adding excitedly, "Do you want to see that one?"

Ralphie, who knew about towers and clocks, had never in all his imaginings put the two together, as in why would anyone do such a thing. And since he didn't know what a clock tower really was, he couldn't help but wonder, *Is it a tower made of clocks?* Or, *How big is it?* And, *How big of a clock would you need for a whole town?* Or, *What if it's dangerous? I mean, what does it run on? What if it's dragon parts—and could therefore be dangerously dangerous!*

Nonetheless, he was always up for an adventure! So, unable to keep the keenness out of his voice, and with a sharp, shrill inflection on the ill-chosen word 'delighted,' he answered as nonchalantly as he could, "Yes … I … I'd be … delighted to see it." And just that quickly, a new adventure was rashly conceived.

"Good! We'll go tonight!" Georgiana then made her way back down the ladder, retrieved the basket of peaches, and hurried back to the house.

All of these new things, like the farmers in the distant fields who hid their food in the open where dragons could get at it without being seen, and the magical peach tree, and his new friend Georgiana, who was now going to show him a clock tower for the first time in his life, and to top it all off … peach pie … left him pleasantly pleased with his adventurous second day of questing.

Life truly is wonderful, he thought as he closed his eyes and nested in the hay, lost in thoughts of peach pie, and peach turnovers, and peach ice cream, and peach pralines, until he drifted off to dreamland.

It was in the middle of just such a dream, wherein he was being crowned His Royal Highness the King of Peaches, and about to receive his bounty of office, in the form of an enormous freshly baked peach pie, when he was startled awake by Georgiana. He didn't know how long he'd dreamed of the Peach Kingdom, but he knew when he woke up that he hadn't eaten even one slice of peach pie, because he was still insanely hungry.

"Come with me!" Georgiana whispered in a gasping voice and grabbed him by the arm. "Here, put this on, you'll need it for a disguise!" At which she threw a dark blue cape with red satin lining and a hood around his shoulders, and once again pulled at his arm without warning.

All of this was rather sudden and unexpected, coming in the middle of his dream, and the cape was rather big and bulky, and when she put it over his shoulders it lay heavily on his wings, which meant he couldn't fly.

"Hey! Wait! Wait! What's the big idea? I can't …" he mumbled groggily, rubbing the sleep from his eyes, and struggling with the cape.

But she never heard his protests—she was on a mission! As they clamored down the ladder together, his paws barely touched the rungs. Which, if she would've just let him fly down, and given him the cape at the bottom of the ladder, he could've done quite more gracefully—thank you very much!

Then, out of the barn, through the courtyard, down the gravel drive, and out onto the rural road in front of her house that led to the town, they ran. When they did get to the road he slowed to brush the hay off his legs, and the bits and pieces that had gotten caught in his ears and behind his scales and between his claws.

Seeing that he was slowing them down, she exclaimed in an urgent whisper, "Come on!" and tugged at his arm again. "There's no time to waste!" she added impatiently.

Who was she anyway? he wondered grumpily. *Why, she could be anybody ... a revolutionary ... even a counterrevolutionary! Or worst yet ... a double agent, a spy for both sides! Or worst of all ... a smarty-pants girl on her own secret mission!* But he wasn't inclined to argue with her, because in the end there just might be a peach pie in it for him—if he played it right.

So down the country road, into the town, and up a cobbled street they went, feet flying, arms flailing, his teeth chattering with cold and some trepidation, as she pulled him along by the arm, all the while trying to explain where they were headed.

"I'm taking you to the clock tower in the square, just like you wanted. We only have a few minutes left before midnight!" And, "Are all dragons as slow on their feet as you? Is that why you have wings? Because you run like a duck?" And, "What kind of flame can you throw? I hope it's got some sting; we may need it if anybody catches us!"

As with all strangers, when it seems like they're helping you the most, they could be leading you into danger. Anybody you don't know could be saying they want to help, but could really be trying to trap or trick you. Ralphie was wary, not of children in general, just the bossy ones. This came naturally to him, like knowing which berries in the forest were safe to eat, and which ones would make you sick. Ralphie just naturally didn't like bossy smarty-pants people, kids included.

So his thoughts began to get scary, and it made him leery, and his imagination began to run away with him. It was well known in Ralphie's village that a lot of people in the Land of the Clock-Watchers were partial to roasted Green Dragon, and that dragon slayers were always considered heroes among the ignorant, no matter the size or disposition of the critter they'd caught.

She's leading me to the town square ... where mobs with torches and pitchforks usually gather! And she's certainly had plenty of time to plot a public pillorying ... and for all I know, all her friends could be waiting up ahead! She could've planned it that way all along. And still no peach pie! Ralphie thought all these things and a million even scarier thoughts on the way to see the clock tower.

But the one overriding thought that kept pushing him forward was how to appease Mr. Hungry-Happy, who by this time, Ralphie sensed, had taken over part of his brain, the reasoning part. So he couldn't help but think, *If getting that peach pie means I have to tempt fate, or death, or destiny, at the foot of a clock tower, then so be it!* Besides, what else could he do? She had him by his imagination either way.

Soon they arrived, and because the town was situated by the river, a fine misty fog had moved into the square, making the gas street lamps glow like small suns—like moon suns, Ralphie thought. Every little thing was wet with dew, so that everything reflected everything else in a heavenly display of a watery world bathed in dewdrops of smaller worlds. It was a magical world without end, endlessly repeating itself in each drop of dew. In every drop on every surface, the clock tower stood upside down and slightly bent, and—depending on which dewdrop you were looking into—made the square structure appear rounded on the edges, which was artistically pleasing to Ralphie, as if the whole square, aglow in the night with the moon suns, were a big, wet painting seen through a million crystal orbs.

The clock tower, bathed in amber light at its base from the glow of the streetlamps, and its masonry brick stacked on an ashlar block pedestal, with its cornice and gables shrouded in the misty heavens, was indeed something to behold. Disappointingly, though, there appeared to be no sounds coming from it, as the crickets tuned their fiddles and the locusts rattled raucously and a lone owl kept up a steady hoot, and underneath it all could be heard a faintly ominous tick-tock, tick-tock.

"That's it! What do you think? Isn't it the best clock tower ever?" exclaimed Georgiana somewhat boastfully.

Ralphie didn't know exactly what he'd expected, but now that he was standing there right in front of it, all he could think was, *It might be beautiful ... but I sure don't think it's anything worth being woken up in the middle of the night for, especially in the middle of a great dream! Even so, I don't want to disappoint her, not after she took a chance on getting caught with a dragon, just to show me a clock tower. Besides, she still might be up to something I haven't thought of yet!* So he opted to say nothing at all, and just stood there in confused silence, peering up into the shrouding featureless mists.

"I'm not surprised that you're speechless! It takes my breath away too! Especially the fancy clock with the little men at the top!" she crowed, pointing to the top of the tower.

"Fancy clock? Little men? What're you talking about? I don't see anything."

At which Georgiana pulled him back from its base, so he could see what she was talking about. And from between the wisps of mists, the top of the tower emerged. Now, as he stood looking up from the bottom of it, Ralphie had to admit it was the finest clock tower he'd ever seen, even though he'd only seen the one.

Still disappointed, because so far he hadn't heard the melody of the bells, he still didn't think it was worth being woken up in the middle of the night for—especially in the middle of a great dream in which he was being crowned king of all things peach related! Except that thought he kept to himself. Finally, with a wistful smile and a shrug of his shoulders, as he turned to go back to the hayloft and finish his dream, he said, "That's the finest clock tower I've ever seen," just to be polite.

And that's when it happened! Before he even got one dragon paw toward the barn, the bells in the top of the clock tower started ringing midnight. Right there and then Ralphie knew, that after that little adventure into the town square with its wet moon suns and pealing, clamorous bells, that he would never be the same again.

Glorious peals of metallic thunder came down the clock tower into his funnel-shaped ears, and through his dragonie body, and out his clawed toes, with such ecstasy that he was frozen solid, mid-stride. Bong! ... Bong! ... Bong! came each new wave of rapture, and Ralphie thought his head was going to explode! But it didn't—it just got deliriously ringy inside.

It felt like waves of sound were racing through his body—thrilling, blissful vibrations running helter-skelter to and fro, at one moment in harmony, then at another in dissonance. An infinite ocean of cacophonous sound waves that peaked and furrowed—peaked and troughed, peaked and guttered, again and again. Ralphie had never experienced musical ecstasy like this before. When he'd heard the bells earlier, when he'd come upon the peach tree, he was at a distance from the clock tower. But now, standing this close, he couldn't move a muscle!

As the electrifying shock waves hit his body and brain, it seemed to freeze him in place, and it suddenly occurred to him that being frozen in place, coupled with his inability to move his wings under the heavy cape, that this adventure to see the clock tower might turn out to be a nightmare adventure! Because in that moment, Ralphie had suddenly realized with complete certainty, that although he was a dragon and could be fierce and fearsome, he did have an Achilles heel. It was that standing so close to clock towers with bells could induce experiences that left him immobile, dangerously frozen in ecstasy.

It also didn't help that the whole time the bells were ringing Georgiana couldn't get him to move either! Which he knew was making it even more dangerous for the both of them. She'd tried pulling him, she'd tried shoving him, and finally in exasperation, she'd even stepped on his tail, all to get him to move—all to no avail!

Ralphie couldn't rightly explain to himself whether what he'd experienced had been induced by the bells, or if it was the way time is felt when standing so close to a clock tower, or had been caused by standing next to a Clock-Watcher girl standing next to a clock tower. But for sure, for that brief span in time—as best as he could understand time—he was frozen solid to the ground, like some sort of dragon statue spell had been cast over him!

Nevertheless, it was one of the most exhilarating experiences that he had ever had. Because these revelations about time, time and music, and the ability of the bells to lift him to heights of ecstasy that'd he'd never experienced before, made him think he was having a Sir Galahad moment right there and then. The moment when Sir Galahad had drunk from the real Holy Grail and was granted his heart's desire of choosing the moment of his death.

Well, if she is plotting with the townsfolk to kill and roast me at a stake, then they might as well do it right here and now, he thought resolutely, because for him this was *his* Sir Galahad moment.

Then, just as suddenly as it had started, it stopped! It just stopped and went dead silent, as if time itself had come to a halt, and then, after a short pause, the rest of the night world began to come out and play again. The crickets picked up their fiddles, the locusts their rattles, and the owl warmed up its hoot, while underneath it all Ralphie could hear the same faintly ominous mechanical tick-tock … tick-tock that he'd heard before. Unfrozen, but still awestruck, Ralphie slowly turned to her.

"Ralphie! Ralphie!" Georgiana cried, shaking him by his shoulders. "What is it? Say something! Why couldn't you move? What happened? Tell me! You could've gotten both of us in a lot of trouble, you know! I was so worried!" She waited for Ralphie to say something, anything, but he just stood there, staring at her dumbly. Finally, stomping her foot in exasperation, she blurted out, "Ooh! You … you're becoming … such a … dolt!"

Seeing the concern on her face, and remembering that she'd tried to save him by getting him to move, Ralphie had to know why. "You knew I was frozen, and you could've run away! But you didn't. Why didn't you?"

"Because we're friends, you numbskull!" Georgiana, still irritated with him, answered snappily. "Why else? You don't desert your friends—everybody knows that!"

For the first time since he'd met her, he saw her as a full-fledged friend. This little adventure, full of danger, in that he'd been unexpectedly paralyzed, and thus incredibly vulnerable to dragon hunters, and yet she'd stuck by him in his moment of frozen wooziness, had sealed their friendship forever.

"Do you think maybe that's what the 'test of time' is all about? Learning how to trust a friend in tight situations?" he couldn't help but ask.

Georgiana scratched her head as if thinking, and then in frustration blurted out, "Maybe … I don't know! What I *do* know is we don't have time to stand around talking about time! It's late, and we've got places to be by morning!"

Still, Ralphie didn't want to leave. Neither did he want to spoil the moment with sentiment, but he just couldn't help himself. So he entreated awkwardly, "Please … can't we stay just a little while longer? I want to remember this night for the rest of my life!"

"No! We can't be wasting time on sentimentality! We've got to get out of here and get you back to the barn before we're found out!" she replied adamantly, starting to leave, but then realized he wasn't following. "What're you waiting for? Come on, slowpoke!"

Then it was the same as before. She grabbed his arm suddenly, muttered some things under her breath, things he couldn't understand—about the numbers on the face of the clock, about twelve bells and midnight, and a new day dawning. They raced down and through the darkened streets. A shortcut here, an alleyway there, a backyard fence to jump to get away from a mad-happy dog, until they were finally back in the barn again.

This time Georgiana let Ralphie take the lead up the loft ladder, staying behind just long enough to make doubly sure the coast was clear, and then followed him as soon as he got clear of it. Once she got into the loft, she placed a few hay bales closer to the ladder to block the view of his bedding if anyone were to come in. Then she kicked some loose hay under the window, so he could lie down on his belly, buried in the hay, and still see what was going on in the courtyard, without being seen.

"This will have to do for tonight, tomorrow we'll find a better place!" she announced authoritatively, her hands on her hips like she was the boss of the world.

So bossy in fact, that Ralphie felt a bit unsure of himself in asking the one question that had haunted his every thought since she'd woken him up. Because, even though it'd been one of the most magnificent days of his life, he really wanted to know where his peach pie was before they parted company. Except that he didn't put it quite so bluntly, so impolitely.

"Couldn't we have some tea? And you know … talk about the clock world … and share some adventure stories … and maybe even have some pie before we go to sleep?" he asked innocently.

"No, I'm sorry, we can't. It's much too late for that. I've got to get to bed! So do you! But don't worry," she said, turning toward the ladder, then stopped and turned back to him. "Look, I promise I'll bring you some pie in the morning—right after my parents leave. Then we'll have all the time in the world to talk about what happened tonight, and make plans for where you can stay while you're here. We have to be very careful—because you know, some people don't like dragons as much as I do! So *please*, try to stay hidden until I can bring you breakfast," she implored earnestly.

Ralphie wasn't exactly happy with that arrangement, but was willing to go along with the delay, as long as it didn't turn out like tonight's slice of air-pie! But before he could think to say anything, Georgiana was down the ladder and out of the barn. So he found just the right spot under the window to curl up in and made a rough bed out of the hay, using the cape she'd left behind for a blanket.

Even without the peach pie, he knew it'd been a great day. He had a new friend for adventuring with, and they'd had a really good time on their clock tower venture. In fact, it might have been one of the best adventures of his life so far, because he had a great co-conspirator.

That night, Ralphie dreamed of the clock tower with its classical architecture. He knew about classical architecture from the books he'd read by looking at the pictures. And he danced in his sleep to the bells in his head, and dreamed of peach pie, and of all things with bells, like sleigh bells and bike bells, along with a bunch of other things related to peaches and classical architecture.

Chapter 3

In Search of Father Time

The next morning came dewy and misty, which made Ralphie nestle even deeper into the hay bed and under the cape. He heard the cow below him in the barn snort and moo, and the horses just outside whiny and stomp, and from beneath the cover of the cape, he watched the grey-striped barn cat climb into the loft, and hiss and growl when he saw him, and then settle himself into the opposite corner, keeping its green-yellow eyes on Ralphie.

Tired and still a little sleepy, Ralphie continued to sleep lightly, occasionally opening one eye to watch out for other animals as they came into the loft—an owl, a squirrel and her babies, and a mouse that was quickly chased off by the cat. Later, when he heard someone just outside feeding the horses, he got up and watched from the loft window and saw a man lead them out of the corral, hitch a wagon to them, and then take them across the meadow and into the furrowed fields beyond.

As he stretched and scratched, and watched everything in the barnyard from the window, he saw Georgiana come out of the house. He watched as she picked up a metal pail, pumped some water into it from the well, grabbed a piece of cloth from the clothesline, and then come into the barn. Ralphie was excited, but since only she was supposed to know he was in the hayloft, he kept quiet, not knowing if anyone might follow her in.

She went to the cow and cleaned her udder with the cloth, and began milking her. As she did this, she glanced up into the loft, and seeing Ralphie spying on her from the corner, put her finger to her lips to give him the signal to be quiet a little longer. Ralphie was wise enough to know that even farm animals would be wary of a stranger in their midst, and if you hadn't been properly introduced, would raise a squawk and a squeak if they didn't know who you were, or what you were up to in their barn.

Having been given the signal, he knew what to do—sleep. After he woke again, he waited patiently and read from his dictionary, and waited and watched, and then waited some more, until he thought he couldn't wait any longer. Just when he'd given up and packed his bindle, and was ready to climb out of the loft and head for the peach tree down by the river to get his own peaches and be on his way, he heard the screen door slam, and dropping the bindle, scurried back to his post by the window.

There she was, with a breadbasket swinging from her arm, and this was his limit! He couldn't help himself because he'd thought of nothing but peaches for so long that he flew down the ladder and out the door before he remembered he was a dragon—and no one in that barn that day, not the cat, the mice, or the cow, ever forgot the day they met the flying dragon from the hayloft.

Suddenly remembering his dragonieness, Ralphie froze mid-flight in the middle of the barnyard, and although not one of them had made a sound up to then, as soon as they'd spotted him hovering in the middle of their little barnyard they began to crow and squawk and oink, and fly around haphazardly, and run in circles, and then, from all directions, simultaneously attack and run away from him.

Landing quickly, Ralphie ran to Georgiana, who immediately put a horse blanket around him. He knew she was hoping to make him disappear as she'd done the night before with the cape, but it was too late—everyone had seen him.

"If you're not more careful, you'll be on the run for the rest of your life!" she scolded, as she stood her ground and looked at each animal one by one.

Ralphie was amazed at how she was able to calm the riotous herd of barn folk, and just as suddenly as the clamorous confusion had started, all the animals went back to what they were doing before Ralphie had come into their court. The truth soon became evident to him—in that little courtyard, Georgiana was queen of the kingdom, the cow her lady-in-waiting, the cat her court jester, and the dog her faithful bodyguard, always walking ahead of her and clearing the way of varmints, gadflies, and snakes-in-the-grass, sometimes not very diplomatically.

She then hooked arms with Ralphie and led him the apple tree in the middle of the courtyard. And just as she'd promised, she'd brought breakfast. Then, as if she'd been bottling them up and waiting for the right moment since the day before the day before, she began to ask Ralphie a million questions all at once.

"Where're you *really* from? I know you say you're questing, but where're you *really* going?" and "What's it like where you live?" and "Who's your father *really*?" and "What does your mother think of you being gone?"

Ralphie wanted to answer, he really did, but he was famished, so he just kept eating and eating and eating, as she kept asking and asking and asking. He was halfway through the peach pie, had downed two or maybe three peach turnovers, along with some peach cobbler and some peach custard, and was about to finish off the sweet pickled peaches when she asked the one question he'd been waiting for, and had wanted to talk about all morning.

"So what'd you think of our clock tower? Did you like it? Could you see all the way to the top of it? Did you see the little men strike the bells twelve times? Did you count?" Then she added, "That's when the new day begins you know; in the middle of the night. Bet you didn't know that!"

With peach guts dripping down his chin, belly swollen to the size of one ginormous peach, sticky from his fingers all the way to his elbows, Ralphie just sat there in silence, not saying a word, because he'd never considered such an illogical thing as the day beginning in the middle of the night. Every creature in the world knows it begins at dawn. But it'd all happened so fast! One minute he was in the loft dreaming, then she'd come in and wrapped him in her cape, and the next thing he knew he was being dragged through the streets, then on into the wet world of the amber town square that was bent at the corners. And then the bells had rung out—who could forget the bells! Then, just as quickly, back down the streets and alleys they went, and back into the barn. So where, in all that confusion, was he supposed to have taken notice of the little men hitting the bells at the top of the first clock tower he'd ever seen?

Still unable to discern what it all had meant, he confessed, "Honestly ... to tell you the truth ... it was all very confusing!" Then, as he licked some peach juice off his claws, he wondered aloud, "I wonder, where do clocks come from?"

"From clockmakers, of course," she huffed. "Everybody knows that!"

"But where do the clockmakers get them?" he persisted.

"They make them from clock parts, of course, silly!" she replied curtly.

"But where do the clock parts come from?" he asked innocently, annoyingly.

"Who knows? Probably the same place as rubber baby buggy bumpers come from, I suppose," she answered, giving up on convincing him of anything.

Having never before in his livelong life heard of rubber baby buggy bumpers, Ralphie just gave her his blank face. "I wonder where you get rubber babies from?" he posed.

Giving him her fed up face, which was a combination of rolling eyes and heavy sighs, she reproved him, "Don't you know that if you show your ignorance by being annoying, you'll get taken for a fool! Besides, we don't have time to answer inane questions!"

Irrepressibly, and not to be annoying, but just out of good, commonsense curiosity, he then asked, "What *is* time?" He thought it might have something to do with the sun, as some of the dragons in his village believed, which seemed possible, probable, and most likely true. "I mean, did the sun make time?"

He asked this as if he were putting a grave and great matter before the both of them, as he thought of his friendly adversary Mr. Sun and what he'd say about time if he could talk. Ralphie knew, in the way all dragons know these things, in his bones, that time had something to do with the sun and the moon, and the seasons too.

"Where I come from there aren't any clock towers because there aren't any Clock-Watchers," he said again, mostly to himself, but thought it was something she ought to be reminded of too. "What was it like in your village before you got a clock tower? Do the little men at the top who hit the bells ever sleep?" he continued, examining the nature of the clock-watching world.

"I don't know ... we've always had a clock tower, ever since I can remember. And the little men at the top, they don't ever sleep—their statues! The bell-makers made them ... to strike the bells on the hour. They're the musical part of the mechanics."

Since he'd already asked about where the clocks and their parts came from and hadn't gotten anywhere, and because he'd been told by the dragons in his village, that the sun had made time, he changed his approach in light of her claim that the day began in the middle of the night. "Do you think there's such a thing as moon time? I mean ... does the moon keep time when the sun's asleep?" He asked these questions out of the blue, without the slightest shred of evidence that the sun had invented time, in this case meaning the daytime, the time when most of the world is awake.

"Time doesn't work like that, silly. There's no sun time, or moon time, there's just clock time—forever and ever!" Georgiana pronounced huffily.

Then he asked what he thought was the ultimate question, the best question of the day. "Hmm ... do we have time to waste asking questions about time?" he wondered, stroking his chin sagaciously. At this he couldn't help but laugh, because he always loved his own jokes.

But Georgiana just eyed him coolly, stating in a flat tone, "Father Time created time." Then, seeing he was about to object, and to stop him from arguing any other preposterous points even further, she used the three most powerful words uttered by all children everywhere trying to back up a sketchy claim—"my father says"—as she went on to say, "My father says an old man lives in all the clocks that ever were! He's really all one person, called Father Time, and he watches how we spend our time." She said this knowingly, like a girl possessed of all she knew, and all that her father knew too.

"Well, that kind of makes sense," Ralphie put forth cautiously, thinking her father could be right. But that still left the problem of sleep time, when people were dreaming, and no one was watching, not even a clock. Because Georgiana's explanation was about clocks watching you, which made clock-watching even more complicated than Ralphie had ever considered.

Ralphie's world had four simple, straightforward, uncomplicated measures of time, Hungry, Happy, Adventure, and Dream Time, which came in random order. So her explanation, while possible, left him with a million other questions regarding time. Then it came to him like a lightning flash!

"My dictionary will know!" he suddenly exclaimed.

That's why Ralphie had brought his dictionary, to understand how the world outside his world worked, and it had never let him down before. Quicker than he could think about it, he was on his feet, and then in flight, and into the barn and up the ladder—this time flying up it, thank you very much, because he had no cape on. Then, tearing into his hobo bindle and grabbing the old dictionary and his glasses case, he flew out the loft window just to show off, and was back under the apple tree with the dictionary propped against a protruding root, on his belly, legs crossed at the ankles, glasses appropriately adjusted, flipping through the pages like the professional looker-upper he aspired to be, at least in those early days of his quest.

By this time Georgiana had seated herself crossed-legged at the foot of the apple tree, and was lazily weaving a coronet of starflowers that she'd found growing in the grass underneath, while watching Ralphie flip the pages out of the corner of her eye.

His little claw flew past the *t's* ... and then the *ti's* ... then on to the *tim's* ... and then, finally, halfway down the page, to the word itself. "Here it is! Time," he said, "is a noun." Then, glancing at Georgiana to make sure she was listening, he added, "A noun's a part of a sentence. A person, place, or thing, you know."

"Of course I know that, everybody knows that!" she snapped. "Anyway, I don't think it's a place or a thing. Besides—"

"But maybe it could be," Ralphie interrupted, "unless clocks only work in certain places, like where clock towers are put."

"Well, I still think it's a person—just like my father said!"

"Maybe—if he's right."

"What do you mean 'maybe'? Of course my father's right—he knows everything!"

So on and on into clouds of confusion they deliberated and debated, without knowing which of the three—person, place or thing—applied directly to their problem of discovering who'd actually created time, let alone what it was made of. All of which created yet another series of questions, such as, when had time begun, and when would it end, and what was to be made of it in-between?

Unbowed, Ralphie forged ahead, reading aloud, "Time—an indefinite continued progress of existence. And events in the past, present, and future regarded as a whole." After summiting that sentence, Ralphie felt both conceptually challenged and mentally mangled.

"Huh? What?" Georgiana asked, looking befuddled. "I don't even know what that means."

"Neither do I ..."

But Ralphie continued reading nonetheless, mostly out of sheer despair, and because his trusted dictionary had never let him down before. Except his voice was getting a little shaky and fading in and out as he continued to read aloud, "A point of time ... as measured in hours ... and minutes ... past midnight ... or noon." With this last definition, he became lightheaded with all the ideas about time in the dictionary, which had never happened before, and his brain soon got woozy as he climbed into the heights of his wonderings.

The idea that midnight was connected to the definition of daytime, and that the past might be linked to the future on a circle of numbers, and that this was somehow connected to the sunrise while the moon slept, mixed with his experience from the night before, that clock towers had mechanical bell-ringers that could freeze dragons, and therefore could be dragon traps, wasn't helping him define time either. And none of what she'd said about Father Time had sounded any more reasonable.

Ralphie looked at Georgiana and could tell from her expression that whatever time was or was not—a person, place, or thing—she thought he was obviously looking for the wrong thing, in the wrong place.

Having given up on reading along with him, she placed the finished circlet of starflowers on her head, let out an audible sigh, crossed her arms, and repeated herself, "My father says—"

But before she could finish, his claws were fingering through the *f's* then the *fa's*, then the *fat's*, then the *fathers* … and then it was only a short distance to the *father t's* and the *father ti's* and then the *father tim's* … and finally, at long last, *Father Time*!

"I found him! Look here!" exclaimed Ralphie with relief.

And there he was, just as promised by her father, Father Time, in all his glory! A very old man with a long white beard and, well, he looked a lot like a god, or at least what Ralphie thought a god might look like. But he was utterly unprepared for what he saw next, because on the following pages there were at least a hundred different sketches of Father Time, each one unique, and therefore the possibility that he could be in all the clocks, like Georgiana's father had said, started to make sense!

To better see what he was pointing to, Georgiana turned and lay next to him on her belly, while he moved the dictionary between them so they could both see the pictures, and with her chin in her hands and her feet idly kicking the air, they reviewed the drawings of old rogues and older gods, and even older trickster gods. In all the pictures, Father Time was old, and so they knew that he'd been around for a very, very long time.

"Look at this one," she said, pointing to one of the pictures. "He's got clocks braided into his beard and hair! And look at this other one! He's wrapped in a dark cape, with the hood pulled over his head, so you can't even see his face … and he's holding something. I can't make it out … an orb of office maybe? Anyway, he sure looks like a mighty shadowy, shady character, to me! Someone that could sneak up on you and—"

"Oh, he doesn't look so scary to me," Ralphie interjected, "not even in the scariest sketches!"

They looked at each picture, carefully studying the details and making clever comments until at last they'd seen enough to make a few suppositions, and even more faulty conclusions.

"He's old, that's for sure! And he seems to only have robes and sandals in his clothes closet," Ralphie observed, as the detective nature in him came to the forefront, blending nicely with his love of words into what he thought was a clever observation.

Georgiana, of course, didn't respond directly, but rather added her own clever comments to top his. "Look at all the accoutrements of office he has!" she exclaimed in surprise. Ralphie was humbled—he apparently wasn't the only one who knew big words for ordinary bric-a-brac. "A stopwatch here, an hourglass there. And look, he's holding a scythe in this one. It's a farm tool for harvesting cereals, you know. We use it for harvesting our wheat. But the way he holds it makes it look like a scepter!"

Of course Ralphie knew that a scythe was a farm tool, and didn't need to be told. But he didn't say so because he was now doubly excited to go on an adventure with someone who had a large vocabulary, and a good imagination too! Ralphie thought adventures weren't worth much if you couldn't talk about them in imaginative detail with fantabulous words.

"Look, look here at this one!" he exclaimed excitedly. "He's got wings like me! And look, in this one he's in a library, looking into a snow globe at a younger man … I wonder what that might mean?"

Flipping the page, Georgiana added, "I don't know, but in some he's so old, all that's left of him is a skeleton!" Which made them laugh.

Ralphie then blurted out, "He's *so* old he'd never be able to catch us, that's for sure!" They both laughed witlessly at that too.

"And look here, Ralphie, there's a whole bunch of family pictures of him with his wife."

They lingered over the pictures of Father Time with his earthly wife, Mother Nature. Most of them were wedding pictures—he was always old in them, and she was always young.

Ralphie observed this and said, "It must've been a cosmic event when they met!" without knowing where that thought had come from, or what it meant metaphorically, metaphysically, or cosmologically. "I mean, look at all the stars in the pictures! And, and all the clouds! And Mother Nature looks so … so happy, almost ethereal." Ethereal was a word Ralphie liked a lot, because it reminded him of his own mother.

"Ethereal? What's that mean?"

"It means ... heavenly ... it means celestial ... it means otherworldly ..." Then, because some words are beyond words, and as he thought of his mother, he said, "It means the warmest smile you could ever imagine!" Which still didn't seem to be enough, so he added, "It's like coming home after a big adventure to your favorite dessert of pancakes with elderberry syrup ..." Which made him lapse into a brain blackout, which lasted a full half of a minute. Then, in final desperation, he added, "It means angelic ... like my mother."

"That sounds like my mother too!" Georgiana sighed.

"Anyway, they both look like gods to me because, no matter the picture," he said, pointing to the various portraits with the second claw of his right paw, "there're always clouds and stars in the background." At least that's where Ralphie thought the gods of time and nature should live—in the clouds, amongst the stars in heaven.

"In some," Georgiana mused, "Mother Nature's pregnant with the Earth, and in others, Father Time's holding a baby or a small child. They're all pretty pictures, but very confusing!"

Ralphie had seen enough to further arouse his curiosity, only not enough to draw anything but sketchy suppositions and speculative conclusions. He closed the dictionary and tried to put the parts he understood together.

"He's old, that's for sure, and he looks like a god."

"My father says he lives in every clock that is or ever was since the beginning of time!" Georgiana repeated maddeningly, matter-of-factly, as if Ralphie hadn't heard her the first three times. Then she backed that up with, "That's why there're so many different pictures of him, I guess."

She *was* a smarty-pants is what Ralphie was finding out, just as clever with words as he was, but as far as he could discover, she didn't own a dictionary—and that gave him the edge, because you need an edge with a smarty-pants girl, to keep her from lapsing into full bossiness. *Plus,* he thought, *for all I know, she could've been sent by the forces of darkness to test my knightliness! She could be an emissary of darkness, an agent provocateur, or a double-triple spy, whose sole mission is to confuse and confound me on my quest for the Holy Grail. Friendship can be a tricky thing when you're out questing!*

"I know! We should go look for Father Time in the clocks in the house!"

Chapter 4

And Trouble Ensues

That's when the trouble started. But at the time, they didn't know that this curiosity about the nature of Father Time would be so disastrous—that was all in the future. They were at the beginning of the adventure, and never considered that this wild spark of an idea, to search for Father Time in the house clocks, could ultimately bring about a calamity, leaving Ralphie's questing in the lurch.

Looking back, Ralphie really couldn't remember whose idea it had been to go looking for Father Time in the clocks in the house. But from the minute they'd conjured the idea, they were under a spell of wonderment, immersed in a conspiracy, and almost drowning in curiosity.

However, in later years, to hear her tell the tale, it had all been Ralphie's idea. "He was always the one with the big ideas! He was the one who'd insisted that we could find Father Time ... if we just opened up a clock or two. Of course, being from the land where there aren't any clocks, or so he claims, he had no clocks of his own. So *I* had to sacrifice *my* clocks! Well, my mother's clock really. All because he'd gotten it in his little brain that he wanted to look in my mother's gold-plated travel clock—my mother's beloved and always-reliable work clock that she depended on every day!

"He was mad with curiosity, I tell you!" she'd often say about the troubles that began that day under the apple tree in the barnyard, when they first went looking for Father Time. At this, she would go to lamenting, gnashing her teeth and making all kinds of wailing and wallowing sounds. Then she'd bury her face in her hands, shedding crocodile tears and looking through her fingers to see if she'd hooked you, put you under her spell in blaming him for everything that had happened after they decided to do what they did.

But it never mattered to Ralphie who was right or wrong, anymore than whose idea it was to try to find Father Time in the house clocks. Because like most of the things he undertook at that time, he was just along for the adventure, as part of his quest, and so away they went.

◆◆◆◆◆

"Come on in!" Georgiana said, opening the back door. "We've got lots of clocks we could look in! I'll show you."

As soon as they entered the house, Ralphie thought he could feel all the clocks watching him. And of course they were, now that he'd been told Father Time was in each and every one of them. Which made him very nervous.

"Over there, that one's called an egg timer, it's for cooking eggs. It's a clock of a sort, I suppose," she explained, as they walked through the kitchen. "And on the wall over there," she said, pointing to what looked like a dish with a rooster painted on its face, "that one makes rooster sounds on the hour ... cock-a-doodle-doo!" They both laughed at that.

Then, stopping in the parlor doorway, she said, "We probably shouldn't go in here, this room's for when we have company, but we can peek in! Look, see over there on the fireplace mantel? That's a clock." And Ralphie saw what was a clock under glass, like a museum piece of art. "It plays an hourly melody too! Isn't it grand?"

Leading him on through the house, she then stopped in the hallway, in front of a tall, narrow, ornately carved wooden box with a door on the front, inset with glass. "This one's called a grandfather clock. I don't know why they call it that, maybe because it's so old. Anyway, it's always slower than any of the other clocks in the house, so it loses track of time from time to time."

Georgiana continued her clock tour, and as she pointed them out, Ralphie lost count—he'd never seen so many clocks in all his livelong life! There was a clock in each of the rooms as far as he could tell, even a clock on the back porch that could be seen from every corner of the backyard.

Wherever they turned, it seemed as if there was a clock watching them, their every move, as well as every move of everyone else in the house, including the dog, all the time. Which to Ralphie seemed a lot like having a warden watching you, wherever you went in the house. It was all beginning to add up to something, what exactly he didn't know. But he could feel intuitively, in his bones, that they were definitely on the trail of something wondrous and ponderous, and perhaps even dangerous, very dangerous, in their hunt for Father Time. It struck Ralphie at that moment, that clocks could very well be dragon traps! That maybe Father Time could reach out and grab a dragon—and trap him in the Land of the Clock-Watchers for eternity!

So, heading back to the grandfather clock in the hallway, Ralphie pointed out, "This one looks like it'd be the perfect clock for finding old Father Time in. It's the biggest clock I've ever seen, so if we look for him in it he won't be so small that we wouldn't be able to see him, and so he couldn't sneak past us. Plus, because he is, after all, just an old grandfather, he wouldn't be scary—and we could just run away! Besides, since it has only a front door, we wouldn't be taking a chance on him sneaking out the back!" All of which made perfect sense to him.

"No, not that one. There's a better one. Follow me," she said dismissively as she walked right past him and went directly into the dining room where she took an old German cuckoo clock, that she hadn't pointed out before, down from a high shelf of the china cabinet. Ralphie followed her, because by then he was swept up in the momentum of the moment.

The clock was a small, dark brown, wooden box made into the shape of a tiny house. She put it on the dining table, where they both could study it at eye level. Ralphie pulled back a chair and sat down.

Kneeling on the chair across from him, Georgiana propped herself on her elbow, so she could use her other hand to move and point more easily, as she began to explain the different parts of the clock, like a teacher giving instruction. "This one's already broken—see, it's not ticking. So I'm pretty sure that Father Time isn't in it, and that means it'd be safe to open so we could see what's inside. That'll give us some practice, before we open one that's alive—that's ticking I mean."

"That makes sense," Ralphie had to admit.

"See this little door in the gable over here? When the clock's working, each and every hour a little bird comes out, and chirps the number of times the hour on the clock face shows." Then, pointing to the clock face below the little gable, she added, "See, the numbers are for the hours, and they go up to twelve in a circle, just like on the clock tower. And since each day has twenty-four hours, the clock hands circle the numbers on the face twice a day. The day begins at six o'clock in the morning and ends at six o'clock in the evening. That means there're twelve hours of daylight, and twelve hours of nighttime. And you've got follow the hour hand and minute hand around its face to know what time it is, not only here and now, but also wherever you were when you were there too."

Ralphie did know his sums, and knew that six and six were twelve, so that if you divided the day into light and dark by twelve, everything she said made sense, but it still didn't add up. *Because,* he mused, *if the day does begin in the middle of the night, as she claimed at the clock tower, does that mean that night begins at noon? And if clocks are in charge of day and night, then how do they tell the sun when to come up in the winter, when the nights are so long? Or when to go down in the summer, when the days are so long? And how do animals like bats, who sleep during the day in caves where it's always dark, even know when to come out at night? How do they know what time it is?* And finally, *And what if you're a fish at the bottom of the ocean, where there's no light at all, would time even matter?*

She then produced a silver key from a hiding place on the clock—a tiny little slot on the back—and showed him how she could wind it up, and how it counted out the seconds, tick-tock, tick-tock. She then put the key in another hole in the clock face and moved the arms of the hands of the dial until they were lined up with the other clocks in the house, which were just about to chime the hour. They waited expectantly, but nothing more happened.

"It's tick-tocking, but the hands aren't moving," Ralphie observed, unable to hide his disappointment. "And why didn't the little bird come out of the gable and chirp the time, when all the other clocks in the house chimed, like you said it would?"

"I told you, because the bird part's broken," she sighed. "That's why they never use it. I guess they just keep it for the memories of where they were when it did work."

Ralphie, in his silliest French accent, then stated the obvious, awkwardly, "Ahh, I see why zees broken clock is perfect to see how eet works! Because eet's already broken ... no? And we would not hurt eet ... no?" He'd often use an inane French accent in joking with his mother, just to make her laugh, or just about anytime he felt like being comical.

But it surprised him as much as her when it just sort of appeared in the middle of their repartee. And when she didn't laugh, and just threw him a stern look, he awkwardly let it drop. But he couldn't help snort anyway, because he loved his inane French accent, even if it was lost on some people. Nonetheless, looking at each other, they knew they were of like-mind.

"That's exactly why I chose this one, you dummy ... so we could see the guts of it!" she added chillingly, as if she wanted to scare Ralphie, like he would be afraid of some clock guts, as if he needed her to explain everything about clocks, which admittedly he did, just not in such a bossy, smarty-pants way.

She then flipped the old clock over and fingered the backside until she found a spring-loaded pin that released the back panel. Inside, the clock was dark and grey and dusty, and Ralphie couldn't see much at first. He pulled his glasses out from one of his scales that he used for a pocket, and adjusted them over his ears, as she picked the clock up to bring it into the sunlight by the window.

The light there was clear and bright, and promised a better look inside. She cradled the clock in her hands, and Ralphie cupped his paws below hers, as they slowly made their way to the window, being doubly careful not to drop it. When they got to the window, they looked at each other with faces full of anticipation at the prospect of mysteries soon to be revealed, and then leaned over the open back and peered into it together. As soon as they got a good look inside, smash onto the floor it went!

They looked at each other, not so much out of surprise, or to blame the other, because they had after all been doubly careful, but rather with wide-eyed astonishment. Because they'd both dropped it out of a sense of ill-omened foreboding, as if they'd seen a ghost, or two or three.

"What … what did *you* see?" she asked guardedly, not really wanting to know.

"I … I'm not sure," he answered, not really wanting to say. "What did *you* see?"

They looked around the room slowly. Nothing in the house moved. Everything seemed to be dead silent, except for the tick-tock of the other clocks as they watched and waited to see what Ralphie and Georgiana would do next.

To any outsider, this moment would have appeared to just be an accident. But Ralphie knew in his bones it was more than just an accident. They'd both seen what they'd seen, and didn't want to talk about it.

✦✦✦✦✦

Later, much, much later, whenever Ralphie was interviewed for the story of his life, he would always say, "From everything I remember—and I'll never forget that day for the rest of my livelong life—it was one of the most frightening experiences I've ever had, or seen! Inside that old German cuckoo clock, there were little people! Little ragdoll people dressed in leather lederhosen and elaborately embroidered dirndls. They were twisted and stuck in the mechanics of the clock—and they were alive! It seemed as if they were screaming for help, but because they were so small they couldn't be heard.

"The distress of it was, all of them had looks of worry and woe and surprise and shock on their faces. Some had been squashed between the cogs and gears, and some looked like they'd been bruised from being knocked around by the hands of the clock. It looked like some had even tried to get away through the escapement mechanism, but they'd all somehow been caught in the mechanics of it, as if they'd been trapped in a different time, seemingly forever.

"That is until we dropped it. When it fell to the floor, all the little ragdoll people that were trapped inside got knocked out of it, running away so fast that they became like wisps of smoke, running under the furniture, under the rug, under the door—never to be seen or heard from again!

"And … and … and this is the part I still don't understand, as they were running, their clothes faded away, and then their bodies became see-through! Then, after that layer disappeared, only their skeletons were left, and then their skeletons turned to dust … and they became like vapor, invisible, but they still had substance too! I mean, you could see their lumpiness when they ran under the rug!

"The only way I can explain it, is that it was like they'd been at death's door—and we'd pushed them through it! And, well, I thought maybe that meant that clocks could not only trap dragons—but could kill people too—and so maybe clocks could kill us in the middle of our adventure! So, like I said, we didn't want to talk about it."

Ralphie also suspected that the broken clock no longer told time the way all the other clocks in the house talked about time, and that's why it hadn't cuckooed on the hour. He thought this because obviously the clock had stopped working at a certain point in time, so that he imagined it spoke of a different era of time, maybe the end of time for them that had been there, then, when it had first been broken.

As he gathered more evidence of what Father Time might be up to, Ralphie was even more certain that things were starting to add up to something ominous, more ominous than he'd ever imagined. First, he'd been frozen by standing too close to a clock tower, and thus been vulnerable to being trapped. And now, he'd actually seen ragdoll people who'd somehow gotten trapped in the gears of time! One thing was certain; his latest discovery in his pursuit of Father Time had opened his eyes to the dreaded, dangerous fact that Father Time could be very cruel. For one thing, he could trap you unto death in bad fashion choices!

He told one of his many biographers later, "Somehow, as near as I could tell, I'd seen into the past through the back of that broken clock. And that's what I'd read in my dictionary, that time was connected to the past and to the future."

Georgiana didn't tell Ralphie what she'd seen that day either, and only much, much later did she eventually reveal it, when she was interviewed for the story of *her* life. And that was best, Ralphie thought, after he'd read her memoir.

"Friendship is a tricky thing when you're on a quest," he'd say to anyone willing to listen. "If I'd told her about the ghosts I'd seen, it could of scared her too much, and we would of had to abandon the adventure. So I knew I had to be brave for the both of us—some things that happen on a quest, the scary things, are better left unspoken when you're in the middle of adventuring—I just *had* to be brave for the both of us!"

As things turned out, and while Ralphie's unspoken misunderstandings about time always seemed to work to his advantage, this little incident would have far-reaching consequences later, as he became more involved with the nature of mechanical clock time versus realer-than-real time. Not to mention, they would've scared the heebie-jeebies out of each other if they'd said out loud what they'd seen there and then! At the time, it seemed to Ralphie that both their attitudes had been aligned—the less said the better, all things considered.

◆◆◆◆◆

Georgiana reached down and touched the clock first, turning it over cautiously, to see what, if anything, was left inside. Ralphie, having seen what he saw, understood why she did what she did. When it was turned over, they double-checked the insides for any loose parts or people by picking it up and shaking it over the table. Ralphie then gathered the pieces that had been scattered on the floor, and together they managed to get the broken clock put back together, as much as you can get a broken clock put back together. After which, Georgiana put it back on the high shelf of the china cabinet and placed a decorative serving platter on a wire stand in front of it.

"There!" she said authoritatively, adding matter-of-factly, "They'll never know," as she de-dusted her hands.

That was close, thought Ralphie, his heart pounding in his ears like drum. *It's a good thing it was already broken before we broke it again!*

Undeterred by the first mishap of the day, they went back on the hunt for the perfect timepiece in which to find Father Time. Ralphie kept any small misgivings he did have about the broken clock to himself during this part of the adventure. Neither of them, it seemed to him, was inclined to entertain random doubts, especially their own, much less anybody else's.

Soon enough, they found themselves up the hallway, at the far end of it, standing outside her parent's bedroom, where Georgiana had become fixated on the folding travel clock on her mother's nightstand. The one her mother used for waking up for work in the mornings.

"Look," she said, as she took the little clock off the nightstand, "let's take a peek inside this one!" Then added, "My mother bought this at Higbee's," as if it mattered.

She then showed Ralphie how it folded in on itself into a nice little square box. "Don't you think it looks just like a little suitcase fit for traveling when it's folded shut?" Then, by pushing a little button on the edge, she reopened it, pointing out, "On the back is the winding loop. And see these dials? They're for moving the hour and minute hands. But to see the insides, we need to unscrew these three little screws."

She never explained to Ralphie why she was so fixated on finding Father Time inside her mother's special gold-gilded clock that she'd bought at Higbee's, or why they couldn't find another, bigger clock to examine, or just go outside and play. So as far as Ralphie could figure, like him, she too was under the spell of incurable curiosity, and once you're under the spell of incurable curiosity, nothing can stop you, not parents, or lawyers, or even a dog like Lassie barking a warning—nothing.

She then did something Ralphie didn't expect. She handed him the clock and asked, "Do you think you could use your claw as a screwdriver?"

He didn't ask any of the obvious questions that would occur to a normal person ... err dragon, because, given what had happened in the town square, they were now kindred spirits, trusted in each other's hands ... err paws, no matter what happened. To Ralphie's way of thinking, that kind of camaraderie was what co-adventuring was all about, and also about having a partner for plotting an escape in case things went sour and they were caught. Besides, who would believe your stories if you had no witnesses?

Ralphie preened at the thought that he, with his screwdriver-like claw, might be essential to unwinding the clock windings. So he put the smallest claw of the smallest scaly finger of his small scaly paw to the task. He'd often used that particular claw to tighten the screws on his glasses, so that when he took the honored assignment he felt not only important and even key to the operation, but also inordinately qualified.

Unbeknownst to most people, Ralphie had quite a skill set in claw crafts. Especially concerning lock picking food larders, disassembly of precious artifacts that he'd been told to keep his paws off of, along with the extraction of lost treasures from sink and gutter drains, mostly wedding bands and earrings, and of course, fixing broken eyeglasses.

But this time, try as he might, the thin wedge of the thinnest claw of the smallest finger of his small paw would not slide into the groove of the screw; it was too fat. Ralphie then tried something he'd done whenever this happened with his glasses. He ran outside and rubbed the pointy end of his claw on a stone to sand it down and make it even thinner, and then returned to the house where he met Georgiana in the hallway by the kitchen.

"Look! I think it'll work now!" he announced proudly, showing her his newly sharpened claw.

But she wasn't interested anymore, as she was headed into the bowels of the basement, on a mission of her own. Cradling the clock in one hand she brushed Ralphie aside with the other. "Follow me!" she commanded.

He fell into place spontaneously, and for some strange reason, he even saluted her with a dramatic flourish, saying, "Yes, sir!" He knew that when she got frustrated enough to ask him for help, his opportunity to be essential to the enterprise would come.

Georgiana was walking faster and with more confidence than a girl who'd just broken a broken clock and lost a few of its parts, thus breaking it beyond repair, should walk. Down the stairs and past the boiler that rumbled worryingly she flew in a flurry, with Ralphie in pursuit. Then on past the coal bin, past the broken bike and the sundry pieces of a long abandoned croquet set she hurtled, as Ralphie slowed here and there, distracted by all the abandoned treasures. Then past an old stack of paintings of her ancestral family by Mademoiselle Vigée Le Brun that Ralphie couldn't help but comment on because he'd seen one or two of them before in his mother's art books.

"You know these people in these paintings?" he asked incredulously, as they all appeared to be royalty, posing in palaces and manicured gardens, all in settings of royal pomp and pageantry.

She slowed slightly, and looking over her shoulder, simply said, "Oh, that's my great, great, grandmother ... and some other relatives. Now quit getting slowed down by every little thing you see! Follow me!" And on into the darkest part of the basement hallway they went, driven by ravenous curiosity.

All this hurrying to and fro did of course make Ralphie want to fly. But he was afraid he'd hit his head on the floor joists above and knock himself out. So he just tried to keep up the best he could, first by fast walking, then loping, and sometimes even skipping, which he knew looked quite silly after a certain age.

The problem was that even with his best loping gait, he could barely keep up. So he had to skip. Which, he thought with dismay, for a dragon looks even sillier than for a person. For a dragon to skip is almost unheard of in the finer social circles of dragondom! Ralphie believed that was one of the reasons dragons have wings, because flying looks much more elegant than skipping, at least for a dragon. No one in dragondom had ever seen or even ever heard of a skipping dragon since the time of the dinosaurs.

And so Ralphie thought, *I'm sure not going to be the first one to break with tradition—but, but, but drastic and scary times call for drastic measures!*

Watching her disappear down the hall into the darkness, his fear finally caught up to him. So that, as he saw her silhouetted against the soft amber glow that was seeping from the edges of a door that opened into what turned out to be her father's toolroom, he skipped the distance between them, lickety-split. Which, as it turned out was quite fun, even if more sophisticated dragons didn't think so.

"This is my father's toolroom," she stated importantly as she opened the door, revealing a small, dim room with one small window that gave just enough light to find the light switch. When she turned on the light, and Ralphie turned in to see what he could see over her shoulder, he gasped audibly.

The toolroom was just big enough for one man to sit on a stool and tinker at a built-in worktable, and for another to stand in the doorway at a safe distance, to give instructions on the more complicated things that he might need extra help doing, like diffusing a bomb, or assembling one, or some such thing.

"He lets me come in here whenever I need to use his tools," she expounded.

"It's a wonderland!" Ralphie marveled, as he looked around at all the widgets and gadgets and funnels and spanners and drills and openers and closers, and all kinds of other tools the likes of which he'd only read about, but had never ever seen before. Some were stored in boxes, some were hanging on the walls—they were everywhere! It was a toy chest for a tinker, an armory full of mechanical weaponry. It was a sanctuary, a madman's secret laboratory.

"Just in case there's trouble, you better go stand over there by the door and keep an eye out!" Georgiana advised.

"Trouble?" asked Ralphie warily. "What kind of trouble?"

"In case something happens to me, and you have to go for help, of course!"

That made sense to Ralphie, so he dutifully took up his post at the doorjamb, as she seated herself on the stool. The workbench was situated along one side of the toolroom, just about the height of the stool, with a swiveling light above it. She pulled its small spotlight into position as she grabbed a hat that had no top, just a clear green visor, and put it on. Then she laid the folding clock flat, unfolding it onto an old dishrag so as not to damage the front lens, and then looked the back over carefully.

"You look like a surgeon getting ready to operate," Ralphie praised her, but she paid him no mind.

"First we gotta get these screws out," she said, like they were bullets in a body. Seeking the right implement, she looked at the shelf above, then to her left, then to her right, searching through old coffee cans and cigar boxes filled with doodads and thingamajigs.

While she was thus occupied, Ralphie snuck the clock away to see if his filed claw worked in the screw slot, but it was not to be. As he was later to admit, he was glad it didn't fit, because to him it somehow limited his liability, given the way things turned out.

After much searching, she procured the thinnest, most miniscule little screwdriver Ralphie had ever seen. The tip was so tiny in fact that it fit the groove in the screw with space to spare. They both stopped breathing as the first screw came out, then the second, then the final last one, but nothing bad happened, which is to say it kept ticking. So she lifted the back of the clock off the front and they both peered inside. This time they weren't looking into the old, dusty, broken back of a broken clock, because the back came off from the front easily, without damaging anything, and the workings and windings of the clock sat proudly on its face, like a small round cake on a glass platter, and all the guts of the clock were right there in front of them, tick-tocking away.

"Oh," she sighed breathlessly, "it's marvelous!"

And it truly was. It was all shiny and gold, and had wheels within wheels with tiny teeth on their edges, and they all moved in rhythm to the tick-tock of its mechanics. Mesmerized by the intricacies of the timepiece Ralphie was instantly under its spell. Under the spell of the engineering wizardry of wheels within wheels, under the spell of springs and cogs and gizmos, and the windings that had so cleverly bound Father Time in such a small space.

Thoroughly enthralled, he watched her study the clock to see what she was going to do next. And when she reached out to touch the big wheel of the clock, the one with all the teeth on it, it was as if he too touched it with her finger. It was then that everything in the guts of the clock stopped, and it took their breath away, as everything in the whole house fell silent once again. And for those few seconds, which could have been hours, it was as if time itself had stopped! But when she took her finger off the big gearwheel it started spinning again, and the whole house started making noises again. First with little creaks and groans, and then with odd bangings of shutters and doors, and it seemed all the clocks in the house chimed and bonged and gonged in relief.

Ralphie could hardly understand what was going on, but it seemed they had accidentally discovered that time could start and stop if you were working on a living timepiece. He also noticed that the toolroom was the only room in the house that had no clock, which led him to even more sketchy assumptions.

Her father could be a Non-Clock-Watcher, trapped in the Land of the Clock-Watchers, Ralphie suspected, further speculating, *His toolroom could even be a place outside the realm of time!* And that was a great relief to him—that such extraordinary places and men existed in the Land of the Clock-Watchers.

So he vowed silently, *Even if someday I get trapped in the Land of the Clock-Watchers, I'll never forget that there're places you can go to whenever you're doing something really important ... like searching for Father Time ... where clocks aren't watching you!*

As Georgiana went back to work on the clock, Ralphie spied, on the wall above the workbench, a picture of a man wearing a silver hat that looked like a knight's helmet, and a special toolbelt. A massive hammer rested on his shoulder, and he was holding a flag on a pole with his other hand.

"Who's that? He looks like a knight of the Round Table!"

"Who?" she asked, then looked to where he was pointing, "Oh, that's my father!" With that she turned back to her surgery again without explaining anything else about the picture, and why he looked so much like a knight errant.

Which, as it turned out, wasn't necessary. Because to Ralphie, her father's hammer was a knight's mace, and the flag bore the color of his heraldry, and so it all began to make sense to him, or at least in terms of his own knight errantry and questing. Georgiana's home was her father's castle, her mother was his queen, she was his princess, and the farm was his kingdom.

Given this, Ralphie knew that Georgiana's father would understand why they did what they did that day, if he ever met him by way of having to explain their knight errant adventure in his toolroom, it was all about a quest.

He looked around the room and found her father's hardhat helmet, which he put on, because he loved hats, and then found his toolbelt, which was too big for him, so he cinched it up and pinned it together with a set of vise-grips.

All the noise and banging that Ralphie was making was clearly annoying to Georgiana, as she scolded him on more than one occasion, telling him, "You're being so annoying! Will you please settle down and stand by the door to see if anybody's coming!"

But Ralphie couldn't help himself, and a few minutes later he'd be back inside the room, pulling more tools off the shelves and out of corners. It was during one of these manic episodes that it happened—and nothing was ever the same for either of them afterwards!

♦♦♦♦♦

As Ralphie later recalled, it went something like this, "She'd spied two more screws on the inside of the back cover that needed to be unscrewed. As I watched the madness of curiosity take hold of her, I was starting to get worried about where it might lead us. But I didn't tell her to stop, because I was curious too, to find out what was behind those two little screws and a half-dozen more. And before we knew it, it, the folding clock, the gold-gilded folding travel clock her mother had bought at Higbee's and used for waking up ... had stopped ticking!"

♦♦♦♦♦

Ralphie was standing at her shoulder, close behind her, when it happened—a spring popped out of the guts and flew up her nose! And with this single punch in the face by the clock she jerked backwards, falling off the stool and into Ralphie. Who had by this time put so many tools on his belt and arms and legs and tail that he fell over too, like a giant metal windmill, flailing his arms wildly as he fell.

Chapter 5

Into the Land Beyond the Reach of Time

The next thing Ralphie knew, the world went black, and then he was outside on a calm spring day looking up at a beautiful blue sky with bright white clouds crossing it. Then a cloud appeared that looked like an old man's face, with eyes and nose and lips.

"Are you all right, my little friend?" he heard the cloud ask lovingly.

Ralphie had never seen or heard of a talking cloud before but he answered anyway, politely telling the cloud, "Yes, yes … I think I'm alright, sir," as he sat up.

He looked at the cloud again, which had by this time turned into an old man with long flowing white hair and beard. Actually, it must have been an old man the whole time, Ralphie thought, and he had just thought the old man looked like a cloud because he'd been lying on his back when he first saw him. Next to him, Georgiana lay dead to the world.

"Who are you?" Ralphie asked, not knowing where he was or who the old man might be.

But before the old man could answer, Georgiana, who by then had begun waking up, groggily asked a question of her own: "Are *you* Father Time?"

At this the old man laughed, and then, in a thunderous voice full of cheer, declared, "No, no, I am the one who created time!" and laughed again.

"What is time, sir?" Ralphie asked, as Georgiana looked on with the same question in her eyes.

The old man asked what kind of time they were talking about. "Are you asking about chronological time or kaironical time? Or are you asking about sun or moon or seasonal time? And let's see, there's also play time, and book time, and theatre time, where time disappears, and a million other ways to see time, which of course can't be seen. And of course there's the time before time, and the time after time. In fact, there are as many ways to experience time as there are people in the world!" He laughed again as the clouds shook in laughter with him.

"Do clocks ever sleep?" was Ralphie's next question.

"Surprisingly, they do. Moon clocks sleep during the day, just as sun clocks sleep during the night."

"Sun clocks? Moon clocks? I've never heard of such things," said Georgiana in wonderment. "I've only ever seen mechanical clocks."

"Oh, yes, absolutely there are such things as sun clocks and moon clocks! But they're not like mechanical clocks. The creatures of the night world, for example, tell time intuitively. You might say they have a clock inside of them, just like you. So just like you know when it's dawn or noon or dusk, and what to do at those times without watching a clock, they know what they need to do between moonrise and moonset, when the sun's slumbering. All the night creatures who live in hovels and holes and warrens and caves, and run around at night, all the faeries and snoods, and foxes and possums, from here to kingdom come, they all live, eat, and play by moon time!"

Then Ralphie asked what he thought was the most important question, "Are *you* a Clock-Watcher?"

"No, only people who take themselves too seriously do that," sighed the old man sadly. "Nowadays most people just follow the hands on the clock, and take time much too seriously, they're blind to their mythic potential!" Then, after a long pause, he added, "Unfortunately, too many people spend the gift of their lives as Clock-Watchers, and so have lost connection with their creative potential. The more they watch the clock, the more they become blinded to the cosmic wonders of the earthly stage they live on, and it's many possibilities for greatness, heroic greatness.

"I invented time, daytime and nighttime and the seasons, to help people stage-manage the epic adventure of their lives. Sun up, curtain rises. Sun down, curtain closed. Spring is one act, winter another. Year in, year out, week after week, day upon day, with every minute an opportunity to be heroic and compassionate and loving, and greater than they ever thought they could possibly be.

"All this could be accomplished if people would just follow their hearts, instead of the hands on the clock! Sadly, they don't understand that the world is a great big stage, and that the realer-than-real world of the Imaginal Realm is within their power to create on earth. So, their role as champions of the good in the preservation of the force of the light, their mythological quest for the Holy Grail—eludes them."

Ralphie didn't understand everything the old man had said, but he thought he understood the old man's affirmation that time, everyone's time on earth, was all part of a great questing adventure for the Holy Grail.

"You mean everyone has a quest? An adventure of their own to live out on Earth—like King Arthur and his friends?" Ralphie asked, because he'd been thinking about the story a lot, and how he could become a king. He'd even latched onto the idea that he possessed the rough handsomeness to be a king or a leading actor, so that acting and staging and scenery and all things theatrical began to dance on his mind all at once, thus he listened even more attentively, and daydreamed even harder.

"Yes, in a manner of speaking you have it right!" answered the old man jovially.

Ralphie preened at the thought that his own quest had just taken on a depth and breath he'd never imagined, with cosmic significance, and since he thought he was on a roll, he asked whatever question popped into his brain next without too much forethought. Which, he boldly considered was the best way to approach the world when you knew so little about it, but was nonetheless sometimes a reckless approach.

"Are … are we dead? Did … did we get pushed through death's door?" Ralphie asked with a hard gulp.

"No, no, you're not dead," answered the old man reassuringly. "You're just in a land beyond the reach of time."

This only confused the matter more for Ralphie, so he asked, "What is death?"

The old man thought about this for some time before answering, "Death can take many forms, and being a slave to time while you're alive is one of them."

His answer didn't help Ralphie understand either time or death any better, so he was at the limits of what he knew to ask and didn't put forth any more questions for a while. But that didn't stop Georgiana.

"Where are we?" she wanted to know. "And how did we get here?"

"As I said, you're in a land beyond the reach of time, the Realm of the Imaginal. This is where *I* live.

"As to how you got here, you'd fallen under a spell of incurable curiosity in your pursuit of Father Time ... and fell through a time portal, and landed here, in the realer-than-real Realm of the Imaginal!"

At that, the old man waved his arm across the landscape and, as he did, Ralphie could hear the animals actually talking to each other, and the chirping of the crickets in perfect orchestral pitch. He looked at Georgiana and saw she was experiencing the same thing. Their eyes were opened to the all the colors of each and every flower, big and small, and they could even see the melody of the wind as the birds flew nested within it. At that first vision of what the Realm of the Imaginal looked like up close, Ralphie and Georgiana were left speechless.

The old man continued, "Now I want to show you something even more dear, precious, and treasured to me than the beauty you see around you, something that speaks to the flowering of your own souls ... something ennobling and emboldening!"

He then turned his gaze to a grassy meadow on a far field. Georgiana and Ralphie followed his instruction and looked to where two knights were silhouetted on the horizon, mounted on horses that blew white smoke from their nostrils. They were so far away that neither of them could see who the knights were, just that they were in full heraldic regalia, meaning they had marks of heraldry on their chests, and flags with crests and trailing ribbons above them. But none of these things had color due to the distance, and so they couldn't tell anything else about the knights, other than they were in full armor and looked like they were about to joust.

They watched with keen interest and quickened heartbeats as both knights slowly began to charge each other, and soon they were galloping at full speed. The gallant figures raced across the meadow and wrecked into each other with a loud crash, falling to the ground in clouds of dust! Both had been dismounted violently, and gave out great groans as they fell to the ground.

Everything went silent after that, just like when the world had stopped in the toolroom when Georgiana had touched the clock gear that first time and the whole house had gone silent. The crickets stopped making music, and the animals quit talking and turned toward the knights on the hill, and the birds rested on branches as they watched, and even the old man fell silent.

Then finally, one of the knights slowly struggled to his feet, but he was staggering—he'd been wounded in the leg. In great agony, he limped to his horse that was standing idly by eating some grass, took the reins of the becalmed beast, and led him off the field of battle.

The old man then turned to them and explained, "I showed you this vision because in time you too may have to fight unto death for something you believe in, just like these knights. You must prepare now, by ennobling and emboldening yourselves. So that when that time comes, it will be the most transcendent moment of your lives."

Ralphie didn't know what to say or ask, because he didn't know what transcendent meant, so he looked at Georgiana, hoping she might. But she just gave him her blank face and shrugged her shoulders. Unfortunately, Ralphie didn't have his dictionary with him, and it seemed she wasn't such a smarty-pants around someone who knew the most important word in the world.

After a pause the old man said, "Your preparation begins here and now. It begins by your beknighting each other—"

"But don't we need a king?" Ralphie interrupted, trying to be helpful. "I thought you needed a king?"

"No ... no king is necessary, not when you're pure of heart!"

With this said, he turned to Ralphie and began to instruct him on how to be beknighted by a friend. "Now, here—let's get you a sword," he said, pulling a thick stick from the ground and placing it in Ralphie's paw. When he did, it magically turned into a real sword, a magnificent ceremonial sword! The blade was fashioned of silver, inlaid with filigreed goldwork along its length, with an ornate handguard of metal lacework, a braided leather grip, and an intricately bejeweled pommel.

"You'll need a shield too," he added, reaching down and picking up a turtle that just happened to wander by at that very moment, handing it to him. Ralphie had often used abandoned turtle shells for shields before, so he knew to put his paw through one end and out the other—but this one was alive! He was already nervously excited and fidgety and overwhelmed, and the live turtle only added to his confusion at first.

The turtle then spoke to him of the proper protocol in how to use and hold a shield in a beknighting ceremony. "This isn't like battle. Mostly I just stand at attention in front of you as you kneel, and the young lady puts the sword on your shoulder and you take instruction. Then, when the ceremony's over, you take me back to your castle and hang me in the grand hall whenever dignitaries visit, and during extravaganzas, of course."

Noticing Ralphie's bewilderment, the turtle further instructed him on how ceremonial shields are different from battle shields. "The best battle shields, as you know, are made from abandoned turtle shells. But I'm what you call a ceremonial shield, because I'm alive—and I want to stay that way. We *never* go into battle! We're used *only* for pomp and pageantry!" With that said he stood on his hind legs at military rest and waited for the ceremony to begin.

None of this seemed unusual to Ralphie, and Georgiana didn't seem fazed by any of it either. It was, after all, a sacred ceremony, and Ralphie knew as well as anyone that talking turtles and wizards can become manifest if the ritual is done properly and in a sacred place, like a vacant lot or a village commons or a magical toolroom, all of which it turns out are indeed portals to the realer-than-real Realm of the Imaginal.

Next, the old man instructed Ralphie, "Here now, take a knee," before turning to help Georgiana with what she needed to do and say to properly beknight a friend.

"Stand here, in front of your friend," he said as he took her by the elbow and showed her where to place herself. "Now put this on." And from out of thin air there appeared a small brown crown woven out of yellow starflowers, just like the one she had made, except with a sheer flowing veil attached to it, which he placed on her head gently. To Ralphie's way of thinking, this made her glow like a real princess.

"Now take his sword, which he offers to you hilt first, and with it, touch him on the shoulder gently. As you do, repeat the words I give you."

With that he stood behind her and held her hand to show her the proper form and said, so she would know what to say, "With this sword I beknight you, and you are forever bound to be true, gentle, faithful, and brave … to let your knowledge defeat ignorance … to be the champion of the right and good against all injustice and evil … and to help all those that need help … even at your own peril … even unto death."

Georgiana repeated each new phrase the old man whispered in her ear, speaking them aloud. Ralphie could see that she appeared reluctant to repeat the last few, probably because of what they had just seen. So the old man helped her again by saying the remaining words with her, as Ralphie bowed his head and listened. "And to help all those that need help … even unto your own peril … even unto death!"

And with that, in a place of no geographical coordination, Ralphie had been beknighted by Georgiana, or maybe, in the metaphysical sense, by the old man. Regardless, he had now become a full-fledged knight errant of the Realm of the Imaginal for real and sure! It was so because the old man, who'd created time, had told him it was so!

Ralphie broke into a happy dance, spiking his sword and doing cartwheels and flying in circles and blowing wispy balls of flame. When he finally realized he was being watched by Georgiana, as the old man smiled with amusement, he got embarrassed, and quickly put his paws back on the ground, hoping they hadn't been watching for too long.

"This is how we celebrate a dragon's beknighting in my village," he told them sheepishly. Which wasn't true, but since they probably didn't know anyone from his village, it could be possible, so he thought it might be believable. And then, to Ralphie's astonishment, the turtle gave him a knowing wink, and then backed up his claim, because by some sort of magic, he had become Ralphie's Groom Extraordinaire of the Chamber!

Next, the old man showed Ralphie how to beknight Georgiana and deliver the same solemn rights and duties and privileges of a chevaleresse upon her, using the same oath that Ralphie had taken when Georgiana had beknighted him.

Then he told Ralphie what to say to her to finish the ceremony for them both, "I will need your help to remind me that I serve a higher calling—to be a defender of the right and good. You are my light, I am your knight."

"Now, give her this." Again out of nowhere, like magic, a bouquet of red poppies appeared and the old man handed it to him to give her. Ralphie gave her the bouquet, and then not by instruction, but rather from his heart, he took her other hand in his and squeezed it.

Then the old man said, "With your friendship you are ennobling and emboldening each other every day with every thought and deed, beknighting each other with your trust and love and loyalty. And by the oath you each took, you are now charged with living your lives in the service of the greater good ... unto ... "

Chapter 6

Returning to the Land of the Clock-Watchers

At that very moment, they found themselves back in the toolroom! Ralphie was lying on his back and Georgiana's dog was licking his face. He was still attired in her father's regalia of toolbelt and power tools and hardhat, and he couldn't get up the regular way. So he rolled to his side and got on one knee. Georgiana, likely having been already awakened by the dog—Red was her dog after all and would have licked her face first—was standing next to him with a long carpenter's level from her father's tool bench in her hands that she was waving around crazily to defend herself. And in what Ralphie took to be her confusion and fright, she accidently whacked him hard on the side of the head. Thankfully, he still had the hardhat on.

"Ow! That hurt!" Ralphie moaned as he struggled to his feet.

"What happened?" they both asked each other, then the dog; who'd apparently come to their aid when he'd heard the ruckus and licked them back into consciousness with slobbery kisses.

They looked at the workbench at the same instant, horrified by what they saw. The clock guts lay strewn all over the operating table, a spring here, a gear there. A couple of cogs and some of the key gears had rolled off the table and lay idle on the floor. For all practical purposes, the clock appeared altogether unfixable.

Pointing out the obvious, Ralphie gasped in horror, "Oh no! It's dead! There's no heartbeat! It's ticked its last tock! You killed your mother's clock!"

"Don't blame me—it's your fault too!" Georgiana shot back. "Why didn't you help me instead of playing with my father's tools? You could've stopped me! Besides, this was all *your* big idea anyway!"

♦♦♦♦♦

During the whole of their adventure, that's the moment when their friendship came under its greatest strain, immediately testing the loyalty oath they had just taken. Whenever Ralphie reminisced about the affair, he tried to tell his side of the story as evenhandedly as possible, given his own liabilities.

"It wasn't pretty. It looked worse than the broken cuckoo clock did after we re-broke it. We must've worked on trying to get that little suitcase clock back together for hours! Of course we couldn't really tell how long, because it was the only clock we'd had to tell time by, and it wasn't cooperating anymore ... since it was dead ... and so we lost track of time, because we were under a spell of curiosity!"

Ralphie would always say this part with special emphasis, over-excitedly, with truth-telling drama in his gestures, deftly excusing both of them from any responsibility in the affair by putting the blame on their mutual psychological affliction, a mental malady that he called "incurable curiosity."

"That's what I mean when I say we weren't doing anything wrong, wrong. We were just looking for Father Time ... and he'd died on the operating table. That clock was dead beyond hope!" He'd say this wide-eyed, without a trace of blame, co-culpability, or personal guilt in his voice—innocently. Because he was now wise to the tricky problems of looking for Father Time in living timepieces, and the bossy tendencies of co-adventurers.

By this time, having experienced the adventure and seen the result, Ralphie knew it wasn't going to be easy to explain in exacting detail to Clock-Watchers, like her parents, who hadn't been there when they'd been swept away by curiosity, just how the folding travel clock had gotten broken by way of looking for Father Time in an adventure wherein they'd actually met the old man who'd created time!

Even back then Ralphie knew that most adults didn't have time for long-winded explanations delivered by over-imaginative children, especially ones with dragon friends! He also knew, that for anyone to accept their story of how the clock had been broken, would require a willing suspension of disbelief—and a vast imagination indeed. So he felt there was little point in trying to explain anything to anyone at the time. Which had made him confidently reckless throughout the whole adventure, as in he hadn't bothered to work out a cover story or, for that matter, an escape plan for a quick get away if caught.

♦♦♦♦♦

The next thing they heard was the sound of wheels turning onto the gravel drive.

"Oh, no! My mother's home!" Georgiana cried out in panic. "You should've been on the lookout at the window too, you bonehead!"

"Bonehead? What do you mean? How was I supposed to know that I was supposed to watch the window too! I'm not a mind reader!" he spat back at her, throwing his paws up in false drama, as he often did when he wanted to scooch away from the blame. "You're the bonehead for not telling me about the window!"

"You should've known! If you're ever going to be a good lookout, you better start shaping up … or … or you can find somebody else to adventure with!"

"But I was just following your orders, sir!" Ralphie countered, shrugging his shoulders and putting on his goofiest smile, as he scooched a little more.

They both crept to the window and watched as her mother got out of the old black farm truck, and went inside the house. Now they were truly trapped.

"Quick, crawl out that window and go to the barn!" Georgiana whispered. "But wait, first we must make a pact to keep this our secret! Even if we're separated and they interrogate us alone." In a tone that told him she was deadly serious, she added, "No matter what they promise, like peach pie for life, you can't speak of this to anyone, ever! Hear me?"

Peach pie for life sure sounds good! Ralphie couldn't help thinking. Nevertheless, he submitted to her instruction with a smart salute.

"Now, take a knee." When he did, she put the level on his shoulder and said, "We're now bound together forever by our adventure to find Father Time. And everything that happened today must always be a secret between us, and forever we will protect this hallowed secret ... unto death!"

"I will! I do!" Ralphie agreed without hesitation.

Because oaths are part of adventures, Ralphie accepted the oath unquestioningly. And the fact that she too knew that it was a hallowed event meant that it was the kind of thing that legendary knight errantry was made of, complete with a witness, and this made him ecstatically happy.

So, with that vow said and done, Ralphie heroically squeezed out the small basement window to save them both. He then took flight around the barnyard, heading for the loft, doubling back when he remembered to grab his dictionary from under the apple tree. Then, flying so fast that none of the barnyard animals saw him, into the loft he went! It was a good thing too, because soon enough her father came back from the fields to finish his chores.

After looking up "transcendent" in his dictionary, Ralphie watched from the loft as her father stabled the horses, put the cow in the barn, watered the goats, checked the hen house for eggs, and then went into the field behind the house one more time to look over his crops before he finally went into the house. For Ralphie it may well have been eternity itself, because up until then it was the longest time that he'd ever had to wait for someone in danger.

As soon as her father went into the house, Georgiana came out, singing and skipping as if she didn't have a care in the world. But Ralphie thought she was probably just putting on an innocent front, to avoid suspicion in the clock killing.

He tried to get her attention from the loft by whistling, but it only came out as puffs of smoke, because all the waiting and worrying had given him a bad case of the heebie-jeebies. When he saw she was cleaning up what they'd left behind hours earlier, the basket and picnic cloth, he wanted to help, mostly because he suspected there was peach stuff lying about that would need cleaning up too. But he didn't dare move from the edge of the loft, because someone might see him. He was playing it safe, just in case.

Thankfully, Georgiana finished up her chores just when Ralphie was ready to take a chance on stirring up the barn folk by flying lickety-split into the midst of them, having spied a large piece of peach pie by the base of the tree. Which he figured he could retrieve so fast that it would seem to disappear. But before he could execute his daring plan, he saw her grab it first and head his way. It was a good thing that she did, or he would have done something foolish, like getting himself killed for a piece of peach pie, and for that he was grateful.

Georgiana returned to the barn and beckoned for him to come down to an open horse stall, where he then sat on a wooden crate and helped himself to the leftovers as she sat down on a bale of hay.

"What happened? Tell me! What happened?" he asked between mouthfuls of leftover peach custard, which was mostly dripping from his schnozzle and from between his teeth by this time, and so he made his questions out of sticky-sounding word noises.

"I fixed it!" she said matter-of-factly ... proudly ... crazily.

"What do you mean you 'fixed it'?"

"I just fixed it," she repeated adamantly, not to be undone with sticky questions.

"You can fix clocks too?" Ralphie asked incredulously. "And not just break them?"

"I put all the pieces in it, and folded it up, and it works!" she snapped scornfully. And then, because he was after all a dragon from the land where there were no clocks, she patiently but exasperatedly went on to explain, "I put the pieces back inside and folded it closed! And when it wouldn't clasp shut, I just used one of my father's hammers and bashed it shut!"

It was clear to Ralphie by her snappy answer that she thought he was asking too many questions. But as far as he was concerned, she was speaking gibberish. "I mean, who becomes a clocksmith by breaking a clock anyway?" he mumbled, which only annoyed her further.

Right then, her mother called her from the back porch of the house. "Georgiana, get in here right now!" came her voice through the barn door and then into the horse stall, and then into Ralphie's ears, shrilly, like someone had stepped on her toes.

"Uh-oh," Ralphie said, as he stood stock-still with peach pie dripping from his schnozzle, saying everything they were both thinking with those two little words.

◆◆◆◆◆

"A terrible fright came over her face," he later recalled. "She looked like she'd swallowed that little clock!

"She looked at me with eyes that were brave and defiant, but guilty and confused too. I mean defiantly guilty and bravely confused," he'd clarify. "But into the house she went anyway, without another word. She looked to me like a heretic about to face an inquisition—and I've seen my share of inquisitions!" he'd share, looking off into the distance.

He'd then further explain admiringly, "Like a girl with her own vision of the world ... a vision that gave her the kind of fortitude needed to deal with imperial inquisitors ... just like Joan of Arc of Orléans!" Then he'd look you in the eyes and declare with unreserved awe, "Her marching back to the house, to face the unknown, was one of the bravest things I've ever seen a girl do!"

On the other hand, to defend herself against some of the claims he made in his memoir, Georgiana later told her friends, "It was completely his fault! If he hadn't had that darn dragon's dictionary, and hadn't been so curious to find Father Time in my mother's special work clock that she'd gotten at Higbee's, I wouldn't have had to face my mother and explain about what happened to her clock—and where all the peach baked goods had gone!"

Later still, right in front of him, for his moral edification and social benefit of course, she'd tell anyone willing to listen a thousand other parts of the story about how annoying he was as a dragon she'd tried to befriend, or so she claimed.

"My life was just fine, thank you very much, until *he* came along—with his little brain, and his big dictionary, and his ways of turning everything *I'd* suffered through into an adventure story of *his* derring-do!" she'd put forth. His side of the story was to her, "Pure hokum ... absolute malarkey ... unqualified gibberish ... he was, in a word, a fabulist!"

♦♦♦♦♦

It was late now and dark enough so that Ralphie was able to follow Georgiana up to the back porch without anyone seeing him. And when she went in through the back door, he quietly moved behind the bushes and around to the kitchen window and peered through.

He couldn't quite hear what was being said between her and her mother, because the window was closed, but he could speculate. "Clock? What clock?" or "Peaches? What peaches?" he guiltily guessed she might be saying, as he saw her shrug her shoulders and show the palms of her hands, the international sign language for claiming angelic innocence used by all children the world over, especially those being held for interrogation for the rapacious doings of imaginal friends.

Ralphie didn't know if the conversation was about the peaches, or the clock, or whatever else she may have been up to in the days before he'd arrived, but he could see her mother get very frustrated as she placed both hands on her hips. He watched anxiously as she then opened the door to the basement, and loudly called for Georgiana's father.

"Fred! Fred, come up here! Your daughter seems to be having trouble finding the truth!" she called into the basement stairwell, so loudly that even though Ralphie could barely hear the words, he could hear quite clearly the exasperation in her voice.

Her father came up the stairs and into the light of the kitchen. He looked at Georgiana warmly and smiled softly. Ralphie watched as her father listened to both of them explain the problem. When they were finished, he just shrugged his shoulders and gave his wife the clown-frown face; the international parents' sign for 'kids will be kids' and smiled a loving smile. Then, turning to Georgiana, he gave her the king's wink as he opened the door to the basement and disappeared into his part of the kingdom, where there were no clocks to break. While Georgiana, seemingly inspired by the king's acknowledgement, held out like a political prisoner, who was being accused of misdemeanors that were being dramatized into major crimes.

Hiding behind the shrubbery, Ralphie followed them window to window, as they made their way to her parent's room in the back of the house. The room where, just mere hours before a lovely, beautiful, gold-gilded folding travel clock had stood proudly on the nightstand by the bed, a little magical suitcase that gave out the correct time for her mother as she got the family ready for work and school in the mornings.

"I'm going to ask you one … last … time, young lady. How did this clock get broken?"

Georgiana looked to be in deep thought—and Ralphie guessed that most of those thoughts revolved around him. But as he listened through the slightly open window from where he was hidden, all he heard her say was, "I told you before … I don't know who did it!"

♦♦♦♦♦

"You see, friendships can be tricky," Georgiana would later say about the whole Father Time adventure fiasco, wherein she'd become a Chevaleresse of the Realm of the Imaginal. She was already the princess of her fathers' farm, and high monarch of the barn flocks, so she was out of harm's way; it was Ralphie that was in a tricky position, life or death wise.

"I could've turned him in right there and then if I'd wanted to!" she'd brag. "I knew he was hiding in the barn, and I could've had my father catch him with a pitchfork, if I'd really wanted to prove it was a real live dragon that'd made all the trouble!

"You know, if I'd have let him, I think he would've holed up in that barn for the rest of his life!" But then she'd think a little deeper and say, "Or at least until the peach harvest was over." Then she'd think a little deeper still and say, "I wish he could've stayed a little longer.

"But, like I said, friendships can be tricky ... and you never know when you might want to go adventuring again, and you just might need a smart, well-read co-collaborator. Besides, I wasn't really lying, lying." At that she'd sigh and look at Ralphie, and he at her, and then they'd both laugh as they finished telling the story of their adventure in pursuit of Father Time in dribs and drabs.

✦✦✦✦✦

"Go to your room, young lady, until you decide to tell me the truth!" he heard her mother order, as she sternly pointed down the hall.

To Ralphie, it seemed that this final act of defiance, even in the face of overwhelming evidence, her having been the only one home at the time, was the limit of her mother's patience, as she had no more words, just a stony expression and a very pointy finger.

Moving stealthily along the side of the house, keeping to the shrubbery, Ralphie followed along outside as Georgiana went back down the hall to her own room. He tried to open her window so he could talk to her, but it was locked shut.

Right at that instant, a monstrous lightning bolt flashed across the sky behind him, and his own shadow was thrown against the far, flat wall of her room. In that moment of high-pitched angst, the shadow looked to him like a giant Bronze Dragon was standing right behind him!

In his fright, Ralphie felt his whole body grow pale, and his knees started knocking too, and he felt the blood drain from his body into his feet, weighing him down, making him feel sluggish before he could even think to run away. And as he tried to stay frozen, so as to not be seen, he even got dizzy for a second or two, and started wobbling conspicuously.

Adding to his tension, the animals in the barnyard flew into a frenzy of whinnies and yowls and cackles and shrieks. Which, he reasoned in his fevered state of mind, was caused by the self-same presence of the shadowy Bronze Dragon he'd just seen. So that freezing in place, and not running away back to the river, was the best he felt he could do; it was neither foolishly brave, nor awkwardly cowardly.

All these thoughts raced through his head in half of a split-second, until a clap of thunder and the hard-driving rain and howling wind brought him back to his senses. The rain, as it fell, outlined everything in the barnyard in the reflections of the back porch light, and there were no ghostly Bronze Dragons to be seen, which was not only a relief, but also a mortification, because he now knew exactly how he would react if he were actually confronted by a Bronze Dragon in real life—he'd either freeze or run away! He'd failed to save the damsel in distress, and this made him heartsick.

After that close call with death, he resumed his tapping on the window, but Georgiana never heard him above the noise of the sudden storm. So he could only watch helplessly as she brushed her hair and teeth, said her prayers, crawled into bed, and turned off the light on the nightstand. The room went dark, and he was left under the window, dejected.

Mortified by the outcome of his first test with a Bronze Dragon, and saddened by his inability to help Georgiana, Ralphie returned to the barn dragging his tail in the mud, crestfallen about so many promising things having gone so terribly wrong. He crawled up the ladder—he wasn't in the mood to fly—and turned in circles in the hay until it was just right in its circularity for his circular sleeping custom. He then pulled the cape she'd given him the night before up over himself, and immediately fell into a deep, dreamless sleep, giving thanks for all things ennobling and emboldening as he drifted off.

♦♦♦♦♦

Later, in his memoirs, Ralphie reasoned that he really couldn't have helped her out. He was a dragon, after all, and most adults can't see dragons, much less hear them. Besides, if they did see or hear him, they might want to trap him! Either way, he couldn't have vouched for her, as he himself was a secret on the premises, and that could have gotten her into double trouble.

♦♦♦♦♦

The next morning was a different day in almost every way from the one before, at least for Ralphie. Not only because every day is different when you're a stranger far from home, but also because the storm had passed, and in its wake it brought the fragrance of fresh mown grass on the wind.

The rain had washed the land clean of its dust and filled the pond in the back of the barn to the brim, and the air was cool and crisp, and not so muggy as the day before. Just like the day before, her father came into the barn, pulled the horses out one by one, putting them in the corral until he could harness them later and then take them into the fields. After which, he fed the cow and the chickens and checked for eggs, as Ralphie buried himself in the hay, trying not to be seen, watching everything from the loft with an eye for trouble.

By this time, it seemed that every creature in the barn was used to Ralphie, from the cat that no longer hissed when he saw him, to the tiniest mouse that brazenly ran in circles in front of him, just to show off. They were all in on the conspiracy to hide him by now, so there was no extra ruckus to give him away when all these whatnot chores were going on.

As it grew lighter, Ralphie watched her father harness the horses and go out into the fields. Soon thereafter, he saw her mother come out of the house and head for the old truck, which had already been piled high with produce to sell in the village, and added some of her homemade cheese, and wild honey, and baked goods to the load. Ralphie knew this because he could smell all of it and more, down to the spices used in the different pies, and the types of butter used for the assorted pastries, because dragons have long schnozzles for a reason—they're gourmands by birth.

As her mother finished loading her goods, along with some sewing she'd done for friends, she called over her shoulder the chores she expected Georgiana to have done by the time she got back. "I'm running late! I overslept—since I didn't ... have ... my ... clock!" She said the last part with added emphasis, to remind Georgiana that she was still in trouble. Then she added some extra chores, "Since I'm late, you're going to have to sweep the porch for me, and feed the cat, and don't forget about the goldfish, and ..."

Just as she was about to finish up the list, she turned and looked at Georgiana, who was standing on the porch. To Ralphie, in his obsession with history, her dress looked a lot like a medieval tunic, and her soft leather boots looked like what a medieval milkmaid might wear, and the broom that she was holding upside down looked like a yellow pennant of battle. In that moment, he thought he was actually seeing Joan of Arc, standing defiantly against the slings and arrows of outrageous fortune.

Despite her defiant stance, Ralphie could tell, even from the loft window, that Georgiana was upset, as he saw her wipe what could have only been her tears onto her smock several times. As he continued watching, he saw her mother walk back to the porch, sit on its edge, and hold her in a hug that seemed to last forever, and he suddenly got homesick, because adventuring out in the real world is a homesick kind of business, and because right about then he could have used a hug too.

Her mother said something he couldn't hear, kissed Georgiana on the cheek, and since she was already late, fast-walked down the walkway, calling over her shoulder a last chore, "And if you can, find out who broke my clock! Who knows, it could've been a bungling burglar ... or maybe it was Red ... or maybe even an angel ..." At this she turned and smiled lovingly at Georgiana, in a way that only a mother burdened with a Joan of Arc kind-of-kid can smile—lovingly, indulgently, and even, admiringly.

Chapter 7

The Back Porch Investiture Ceremony

Ralphie waited in the loft for what seemed like forever before Georgiana finally came to the barn to milk the cow. As soon as she did, he flew down to be beside her. The cow only slightly noticed him as she looked up from her feeding trough, hay stuck in the corners of her mouth, and to Ralphie, she seemed to nod a friendly hello, before going back to her chewing.

He could tell Georgiana didn't want to talk, so he just nuzzled against her shoulder, making his concern known, without demanding her full attention. He could feel her sadness in his bones, and for him that was what friendship was all about, because after the adventuring, after the spills and chills and fun and danger that every adventure entails, it was about the friendships you found along the way. A closeness where the two of you become almost of one mind … a sensing of each others' feelings, not needing words … the fondness you found you had for someone that you really liked to go adventuring with. They were keen on each other that way.

Georgiana almost started crying when, in hope of comforting her, he finally said, "I understand about the clock being broken and all, but we could make reparations … no? I could get a job … paperboy maybe, and we could buy another clock, and at the same time we could harvest more peaches and bake more pies to sell."

But alas, unbeknownst to him, the problems for her were mounting up. Because for some odd reason, despite having played with the children of the Clock-Watchers before having left his father's kingdom on his own quest, it hadn't directly dawned on Ralphie that having a dragon for a best friend that you spent days and days with, but could never talk about, would be so tricky.

"I don't have the words," she sighed sadly.

"I know," he agreed, not really knowing what she meant. "I don't either," he added, because it seemed the sympathetic thing to say, still not knowing what she meant.

"You're going to have to leave."

At this Ralphie jerked back, like he'd been scalded. "What? Leave? Are you sure?" he gasped, somewhat aghast. "I mean ... I just got here! I don't even know you very well yet ... we could be lifelong friends ... and if I leave now we'll never know!" He started pacing around the stall, arms and tail flailing, his voice getting shriller with each proclamation.

Georgiana watched wordlessly, as he wound himself up by walking in circles and babbling mindlessly. "We could've been a great team, you and me, you know? I mean, you really got guts, sister! And now what's to become of us?" Although Ralphie knew in his bones that he was pushing against fate, he just couldn't stop. "What am I supposed to do now? Go out and find another well-read musketeer, just like that? We could've been contenders ... we could've become legends of our own, you and me! Why, we could've ruled the world from right here, and this cow could've been part of our court, minister of all things dairy related! And Red, your dog, could've been our prime minister of foreign affairs! And those pigs could've been our—"

To put an end to his frenzy, Georgiana simply reached out and hugged him, like her mother had hugged her, and told him, "Since I don't have my own words, I'll tell you what my mother just said to me ... 'You know I'll always love you, down to your littlest bone!'" Then, to ease his hurt a little more, she added, "You can always come back, you know ...

this could be your haven if you ever got wounded in a questing battle. It's just that you can't stay today … and you best not come around for a while."

This seemed odd to him, if she truly did cherish his friendship. But he was learning that he'd have to make allowances for minor flaws, fabrications, and outright fibs in the truth-telling department if he wanted to adventure with anyone who wanted to go on adventures with dragons, especially if they were trying to spare your feelings. He looked it up later in a library, under dragon-related relations with Clock-Watchers. It was called "being tactfully tactful," or "minding your words," or in the worst case, "being diplomatically duplicitous." But he knew from what his mother had told him, that it was of utmost importance that he be high-minded about the intentions of his co-adventurers.

Apart from what she'd said, Georgiana didn't need to say much more. Because what was most important about their adventure was that they'd spent time in the Realm of the Imaginal. So her telling him that he had to leave, whatever murderous perils might ensue, didn't really matter. Because to his way of thinking, they had accomplished their quest, they had found the old man who'd created time, which was better than finding Father Time. And now that it was over, he imagined that she was doing what she thought was best for the both of them.

And now, because they knew the secret of the toolroom without a clock, and the dangers of getting caught up in incurable curiosity, it was clear that if they stayed together it could be more dangerous for him, given that they were both ardent adventurers, because it would increase the likelihood that Ralphie would get caught eventually!

High-minded sentimentality aside, Ralphie did his best to ignore his hurt feelings and see the silver lining. He had seen things in that little toolroom that gave a place and space for his imagination to roam. And for him, that held the promise that when the time came, he could find a time portal to his home, back to the Land of the Non-Clock-Watchers.

Still, no matter how diplomatic Georgiana had tried to be, and in the midst of all the other demands on his fortitude, Ralphie found himself fighting a sinking feeling that he was being forced into exile, without a retinue, just like his father had been. And maybe even, just like his father, be left vulnerable to assassination, being so far away from home.

But at that moment he was more focused on having to leave Georgiana than on being exiled, or on random assassination attempts, or even on returning home. He didn't want to say goodbye, so he just stood and looked at her, eyes blurry with tears, making her look like she was formed out of watercolors. He reached out and hugged her to make sure she was real. In doing so, he was surprised at how small she really was. Even though she was about his age and size, he'd always thought of her as bigger, maybe because she was such a bossy smarty-pants.

As he fought against his own sadness, he couldn't help but wonder, *Who's going to help her on her next adventure? Who'll protect her ... if not me?* as a thousand other unspoken sentiments bound in mutual concern seemed to hold them together, in a timeless moment of unconditional surrender to their friendship.

He could feel that she did not want to say goodbye either, because she was still hugging him too. But eventually, she pulled away, straightened her shoulders, drew a deep breath, and with a tremble in her voice, sighed softly, "Oh Ralphie, I don't want to lose the best friend I could've ever imagined!" Then, after another shaky breath, almost as if to strengthen herself against dragons with demented dreams, she quietly murmured, "I have to go now. I have chores to do." And with that, she kissed him on the side of his schnozzle, and headed back to the house at a determined trot.

She was halfway to the house when Ralphie called out, "Wait! Wait!" catching up with her when she'd reached the porch.

He didn't want to part without leaving her with some kind of keepsake to keep safe his memory, and to say goodbye without saying goodbye ... he wanted to be friends for life. So, like a medieval knight errant prince might leave a locket with his portrait for inspiration, a seed of love for his chevaleresse to plant in her heart, Ralphie wanted to give Georgiana something to use in her own magical imaginings. And so, because his friends had always told him that dragon scales are said to be magical for Clock-Watchers, he gave her a scale, a magical dragon scale.

Digging in his pockets, he retrieved a small scale that had fallen off the night before. Holding out his paw to show her, he said, "This is for you ... it's magical."

The truth of it was, Ralphie didn't really know what dragon magic could be made of it, because scales weren't magical for dragons. But nonetheless, he didn't want to part from her without leaving behind some kind of enchanted charm to help her dream of him.

She looked into his cupped paw and gazed down upon the scale. "Magical? What's it for? What's it do?"

Ralphie had to think fast, because he didn't really know for sure. "This one's connected to me by my dreams," he told her. "If you keep it with you, you can spend time with me in your dreams. And you can see what I'm doing … and where I live … and who my friends are … and even whatever quest I'm on! And we can keep going on adventures together forever!"

Thrilled at the thought of adventuring together in their dreams, and filled with anticipation, Georgiana blurted out excitedly, "Maybe we could go back to the Land Beyond the Reach of Time—back to the Realm of the Imaginal!"

Realizing that his claim of it being magical had been accepted at face value, he unleashed his imagination further by making a second, even more outlandish claim. "And if you can make yourself very, very small, as small as a teardrop, and put yourself in the middle of it, the whole world will change in radiance and beauty! Because, like I said, it's connected to me through my dreams."

With that, he handed it to her, and as he did, she shed a few tears, and as she was wiping them away, still holding the scale cupped in her hand, her tears hit the scale, and then it happened!

"Ralphie! It … it really works! Everywhere I look … the world's changed! My house has turned into a great manor … and the barn's now a coach house! And … and the whole barnyard's paved with cobblestones! Why, the whole farm's become a beautiful estate with manicured gardens!" Then, turning to Ralphie, her eyes got really big and she swooned admiringly, "And you ... you ... oh, Ralphie ... you really *are* a prince!"

Ralphie didn't know what dragon magic had happened to her, so he was somewhat nonplussed when she said what she said. "Of course I am!" he answered adamantly. "I already told you that when we first met!"

♦♦♦♦♦

Some years later, when writing her memoirs, Georgiana explained how the miraculously magical changes had come to pass. "Once my tears touched the scale in my hand, somehow by magic, just as he'd claimed, the whole world changed in radiance and beauty! To my complete surprise, I suddenly found myself in the courtyard of a medieval manor, even though I knew it was still my family's farm.

"But even more amazingly, right before my eyes, Ralphie had turned into a confident, handsome, armor-clad knight errant! A hero right out of every fairytale adventure story I'd ever read or heard about! But then, when he spoke, the spell was broken ... and everything changed back. And since I was happy, I couldn't cry anymore, so I knew I'd have to wait until I really missed him, for the magic to work again."

♦♦♦♦♦

"Oh, Ralphie, this truly is the best gift I could ever imagine," she exclaimed in wonder. "I'll treasure it forever! Thank you!" She then held the scale up and examined it carefully, before putting it in a hidden leather pouch tucked under her belt. "This is where I keep all my most treasured treasures! I'll keep it with me forever!" Then she suddenly exclaimed, "Wait! Wait here!" and ran into the house like she'd been struck by a bolt of lightening.

Ralphie waited by her back porch like the Green Dragon on the loose that he was, for the entire world to see. A Green Dragon on the loose and in the open—in the open where any random rube just happening by could see him and start trouble. To be hunted without mercy and tied to a stake, to be roasted alive by uncultured savages with pitchforks and torches who had probably never heard of, much less read, a dictionary! He was, after all, in the Land of the Clock-Watchers, where all the great battles on the war on ignorance were fought.

Nonetheless, at that moment, the most troubling question that crossed his mind was just how long saying goodbye to someone you thought you could be life-long friends with, and may never see again, could take in real-life. Given that he wanted to live long enough to quest his way to the Holy Grail.

He thought this and many other scary thoughts as he waited and waited and waited for her. This overlong waiting created all kinds of unwarranted drama for him. But because by now he trusted her implicitly, he was willing to deal with the danger as best he could—with an array of nervous ticks—tapping his toes and cracking his knuckles while whistling nervously off-tune. In short, the waiting was making him antsy.

Georgiana finally returned with a talisman of her own to send him off with. It was a silver medal with a horse on it called *The Beautiful Jim Key*. The medal swung from a silver bar that said "Mercy Pledge Member." On the back of it was the Jim Key pledge of fidelity that read, "I promise to be kind to all harmless living creatures and protect them from cruel usage."

"You can wear it on your chest after you take the pledge!" she said as she showed it to him.

Ralphie was about to accept this great honor by thrusting his chest out, but she held back, whispering in his ear, "You must kneel down first." So he knelt down as instructed, just as he'd done in the Land Beyond the Reach of Time.

At that, she picked up a shepherd's crook that her father used for moving livestock, placed it on his shoulder, and proclaimed with great pomp and circumstance, "With this sword, I bestow upon you the accolade of knighthood!" But then she paused.

At first, Ralphie thought she was just gathering her thoughts, or perhaps she was pausing ceremonially, dramatically, theatrically. But whatever the reason, it didn't matter, because either way, the longer they loitered, the more dangerous it was becoming for both of them. Which made Ralphie begin to wonder what he'd gotten himself into. *What's she waiting for? Maybe I don't want to get involved in any more dangerous adventures anymore ... and maybe I don't want to take any more oaths—especially ones that involve oaths of fidelity unto death!*

Finally, just as he was getting ready to scooch away from taking any more death oaths, she said softy, under her breath, "I can't remember all the words to use. You might have to help me."

So after some reminding from Ralphie about the ritual from the day before, she continued confidently, "With this sword I beknight you! And you are forever bound to be true, faithful, and brave ... to defeat ignorance ... to be a champion of the right and good against all injustice and malevolence ... and to help all those that need your help ... no matter the risk!" Then after a few more vows involving courtly folderol, she sealed the oath with the dreaded final pledge, "Unto death!"

Ralphie was flabbergasted! Although she'd forgotten some of the words, she'd remembered even more than he did of the beknighting ceremony from the land beyond time. Despite his occasional doubts over the last few hours, as to whether it had all been a dream, or maybe that his imagination had run away with him again, or maybe that he'd lost his marbles, now there was no mistaking whatsoever that what'd happened in her father's toolroom had happened to them both. They were each other's witnesses that they had indeed gone to a land beyond the reach of time, to a place that was realer-than-real—the Realm of the Imaginal!

Georgiana then proceeded as before to bestow the solemn rights and duties and privileges of Errant Knighthood upon Ralphie. She remembered these rights and duties from the ceremony in the land beyond time, of course, but added a few more because, according to her, like Ralphie, many of her relatives were of royal descent.

"As a knight errant, you have the right to fly your own banner beneath that of your served lord. You're also permitted to wear your own colors into battle. And when not wearing your armor, you must wear the most fashionable fashions!"

Ralphie glowed and smiled and nodded in agreement at this obligation, because he loved courtly costumes and capes. Especially fancy hats.

"As a knight errant, you are also awarded favored treatment in the eyes of the law. That mostly means that you can hunt on the king's properties without penalty."

He already did this of course—he was a true dragon prince after all, and not subject to the illegitimate king's edicts anyway—so he just nodded and smiled indulgently.

"As a knight errant, you're also required to enforce the laws of the kingdom. Mostly that means that if you're called upon to serve your lord, you must do your honor bound duty! And I'm sure I don't need to remind you that as a knight errant you're sworn to valor, and vow to fearlessly confront the forces of darkness, even when it may bring about your own death!"

Ralphie gulped hard at the mention of this death oath again, as he did whenever death was mentioned, especially his own, and wondered why she kept bringing it up.

"Finally, you pledge that your honor-bound duty as a knight errant is to serve the Transcendent!" She had looked it up too. "And, oh! I almost forgot—you also agree not to beat up random members of the clergy! And here's the best part! If you get killed in battle, as a pledge from all proper knights to all praiseworthy knights, we promise to have a statue of you in full armor made for your mausoleum. Think of it, Ralphie! You'd be immortal!"

"You would? I *would*? Yes! I'll do it!" he said most earnestly.

"You were supposed to repeat the words, Ralphie!" she admonished.

Which he couldn't do because he'd already jumbled them all up in his mind. Nonetheless, he tried his best, "I promise not to randomly beat up people wearing unfashionable clothes … and to get a statue of myself made in full armor for museums … and to never run away from darkness … except when death is at the door!" He added the last part sotto voce, under his breath, because he reasoned, *How could I serve the Transcendent if I'm dead?*

With that, right there and then, Georgiana clasped the Jim Key medal around one of his scales, had him hold his right paw in the air, then asked him to repeat, as best he could, given what had just happened, the *Jim Key Mercy Pledge* to seal the deal.

"I promise ... to be kind ... to all harmless living creatures ... as long as I live," he said hesitatingly, because he couldn't quite remember all the words. Then added, "And furthermore, to protect them from cruel usage ..." He hesitated again, hoping that was enough to satisfy her. But after a grave look and arched eyebrow from her, he gulped hard and finished strongly, "Unto death!"

He said this with pride bursting out of his solemnity, so much so that Georgiana got caught up in his enthusiasm, and lifting her arms up in the air, boldly commanded, "Go forth, Sir Ralphie, and conquer the hearts of all the people across the land with chivalric derring-do and courtly folderol, and all things related to polo matches and puppet monarchies!"

At that, Ralphie did his happy dance and celebrated by spiking his shepherd's hook sword, and doing cartwheels and flying in circles and blowing wispy balls of flame. Meanwhile, on the ground, Georgiana joined him in his celebrating, laughing and clapping, and turning somersaults and twirling until dizzy, with Red barking and jumping and dancing alongside her, until all three finally collapsed in happy exhaustion.

Then, almost as if on cue from the gods that write beknighting ceremonies into legend, Georgiana stood up and took from her pocket the sweetest, most beautiful peach Ralphie had ever seen, and handing it to him said, "This is the orb of office of the philosophical kingdom you are to reign over henceforth! It's part of your regalia of office."

Just as he was about to take a bite of it, she added sternly, "But whatever you do, do … not … eat … it! It's magical!" And then she continued, "Henceforth, you will forever be known as Sir Ralphie the Great … Knight of the Kingdom of the Peach Orchard … and the Realm of the Imaginal too!"

By the time the beknighting ceremony was over, Ralphie was finally and totally convinced that he was indeed not only a self-declared knight errant in his own right, and of the courtyard ceremony of the Peach Kingdom, but best of all, of the Realm of the Imaginal, as well.

As he looked around, he thought he heard most all the animals in the barnyard court give their approval with a couple of whinnies from the horses, a loud moo from the cow, and saluting snorts from the pigs. But then again, he was somewhat fanciful when it came to courtly folderol. It had been a great day in his life, maybe the greatest, so he felt he was entitled to poetic license!

"Now do me!" she instructed him.

Ralphie changed places with her and got on the porch, as she stepped onto the ground, and using the shepherd's crook she had used, placed it on her shoulder. "With this sword I beknight you. Henceforth, you shall be known as Lady Georgiana, Chevaleresse of the Kingdom of Peaches!" he pronounced theatrically, imperiously, swashbucklingly.

"And the Realm of the Imaginal too!" she whispered insistently.

Not to be undone, Ralphie dutifully added, "And the Realm of the Imaginal too!"

Then, to finish the ceremony for them both, he took her hand and pulled her onto the porch, and added loudly, so all the barn folk could hear, "I am your knight, and you are my light!" and was quite pleased with himself.

Georgiana reached out and took his paw in her hand and squeezed it silently. This was not part of the ceremony, but rather it came from her heart.

Ralphie got embarrassed easily, especially when he ran out of words for saying sentimental things to someone he loved so much, so all he could think to say in response was, "I have no words …"

"I know. I don't either." Again, for the second time that morning, she couldn't find the words to say how she felt in her heart for Ralphie and his endless entertainments, which had made their adventure quite wonderful. Ralphie was glad she couldn't, because he was out of words too.

With that said and done, after another long, heartfelt hug, they parted, she back into the house, and he back to the barn. Then, after collecting his dictionary and glasses and other sundries from the loft, Ralphie simply slipped out the back of the barn and down the trail to the peach tree. After plucking a few ripe ones and putting them in his bindle, he melted back into the forest that lined the riverbank.

All in all, Ralphie thought as he walked away, it had been a wonderful adventure! Even though they hadn't found Father Time, they had fallen through a time portal in her father's toolroom and into the Realm of the Imaginal where they'd met the old man who'd created time. Which showed Ralphie that there were places in the world of Clock-Watchers where time disappeared, where you could travel to places beyond the reach of time, and her father had made just such a time portal—and *that* was much more important than anything else they could have discovered!

The Auparavent

What Came Before

On nights when they weren't talking about family ancestry at the dinner table, they would often talk about the Chivalric Code, or the Order of the Heart, or the quest for the Grail, or most importantly, the usurpation of Ralphie's rightful birthright. These discussions were often played out in mock-theatrical productions, and in the theatre of all of this suppertime story-play, the breastwork needed for a philosopher prince was being carefully laid, word-by-word, evening-by-evening, in never-ending conversations between Ralphie and his mother.

The following are just a few examples of the many conversations that had taken place each evening before Ralphie left on his questing adventure, where a few basic philosophical questions were asked ... a million different ways. For succinctness, these conversations are described as having happened during one meal, on one evening.

❖ ❖ ❖

"Tell me again about how the Dragons of the Verbose made history and changed the world, Mama," pleaded Ralphie. "And how everything the world knows about chivalry would've been forgotten, if it weren't for the legendary Knights of the Order of the Heart!"

Pausing from stirring the large cast iron pot with its steaming contents, she smiled and looked at him with her big violet eyes, framed with long, double-rowed lashes, the pale green of her face rosy from the heat, and stepped back from the fireplace, wiping her paws on her apron, before checking the biscuit dough, and putting it in the firebox.

His mother was a smaller dragon, green of course, with delicate features and a shorter snout than most, and skin that was soft as velvet on her paws and face and belly. But for Ralphie, her finest quality by far was her smile. It had a redeeming eminence, a way of giving whomever she smiled at their full dignity. As if she could never think ill of anyone, no matter how mean or nasty they were rumored to be. Her smile, not her rank as an exiled princess, set a court of its own, in which all were accepted, including misfits and miscreants, with respect and dignity—and most importantly, unconditional love. In a word, her smile was ethereal.

"You want to hear about the Dragons of the Verbose and the Order of the Heart *again*?" she asked, amused, as Ralphie nodded his head eagerly.

"All right," she sighed. "Well, as you know, the wars on ignorance have been fought for millennia by the Dragons of the Verbose. And the legends of the Order of the Heart are about a very extraordinary group of Green Dragons who were working especially closely with mankind in changing the destiny of the Clock-Watchers' world for the better.

"Long before they were ever born, the fates of many of these legendary knights were tied to the Great War on Ignorance—it was their calling! And, just like your father, they fought tirelessly against the violence of ignorance, through their heroic, selfless acts of grace."

"With lots of derring-do and swashbuckling too!" Ralphie chimed in, jumping up from his chair and running to the fireplace, where he grabbed the fire poker, and then, as if he were sword fighting, he swashbuckled around the room with it, jumping on furniture, sliding on rugs, then out the large front window, where the rock had been rolled back, and out onto the terrace, where a hundred other imaginary foes lay in wait for him.

"Put that poker up and get back in here and settle down!" she called out after him. "How many times do I have to remind you? It's not all about sword fights and fancy footwork!"

Somewhat downcast at her words, Ralphie reluctantly came back inside, dragging the poker, which he put up with a double slash flourish before returning to the table and sitting down.

Once he was settled, she drove home the point, emphasizing her words with the wooden spoon, pointed in his direction. "You may treat all of this like it's just a big, make-believe adventure, Ralphie, but you should never forget who you're descended from—that your ancestral stock includes knights and lords, and shamanic priests and warrior writers, and celebrated artists, and even some notorious flaneurs too— therefore, much more is expected from you than from the average Green Dragon!"

This was something Ralphie had heard many times before. And whether her stories about his ancestry were imagined or real, she reminded him of his grand heritage so often that he could name a hundred great thinkers and doers who he believed were somehow related to a branch of his family tree, and sometimes him in the particular, right off the top of his head.

"Those of the Order of the Heart," continued his mother, "instead of resorting to violence, strove to keep the Chivalric Code of non-violence alive. Not only by living it, but also by trying to prevent violence through the stories they wrote and the plays they put on. Starting with the theatrics of our family's very own ancestors, the Troubadours of Languedoc!

"The Order also influenced the culture of the Clock-Watchers through the invention of the printing press, and through the great libraries they built and opened to all kinds of readers—regardless of their station in life. Why, they even helped establish academies throughout the enchanted forests that border the Land of the Clock-Watchers, all run by the finest professorial Green Dragons in all the lands, for the training future philosopher kings!

"Over the years they've worked tirelessly to fulfill their charge of keeping the light of chivalric grace and mercy alive in the darkness of an ignorant and cruel world. They sacrificed much ... some of them even unto death," she finished, her voice filled with pride and sorrow and dread, all at the same time.

"But I'm not afraid to fight my half uncle, he's a traitor!" objected Ralphie heatedly. "Or even any of the traitors at his court either! Or anyone else who's ever fought against the Order of the Heart! Even the Bronze Dragons if I have to ... even unto death!

"But don't worry, Mama, they'll never get me!" he finished with reckless confidence, emphatically, braggadociosly, picking up a butter knife and pretending to stab his treacherous half uncle by stabbing a loaf of bread to death. Which led to his imitating his half uncle's ghastly demise, which included a rolling of the eyes, great groans and gasps, along with some dramatic flailing about in his wingchair. All of which he cheerfully enacted for her benefit; it was, after all, his birthright that was at stake!

Smothering a smile at his endlessly entertaining derring-do antics, and stopping momentarily to taste a bit of the stew and pronouncing it almost ready, she turned down the fire to let it simmer, and told him, "You know, Ralphie, these stories I share with you always come down to one thing." She then reached over for some preserved toad toes, which she kept in a pickle jar, in a row of pickle jars of oddly named mushrooms, including dead man's fingers, wood ear, bleeding tooth, and octopus stinkhorn, and added some to the stew, along with a dash of her secret spice blend, the rich, earthy aroma of which always reminded Ralphie of the freshly cut larkspur that grew abundantly in the forest.

Then, after another quick taste, she continued, "As you know, I want you to follow in your father's footsteps and become, like him, not just a prince by birth, but a philosopher too! I want this for you, Ralphie, more than anything … just like your father wanted it for you!" A soft luminescence flickered across her face and down her scales at these words, and a gentle softness came into her voice.

Ralphie thought this was one of the most beautiful things about his mother, how her scales would luminesce whenever she spoke of his father, as if she were aglow with warmhearted memories. At this he always knew an adventure story about his father was coming, as she would often appear flush when getting ready to regale him with adventurous tellings involving his father's many escapades.

These tall tales often blurred the line between fact and fiction, between the truth and the imaginal, between the real and the realer-than-real, and Ralphie never tired of hearing them, and on this particular evening, he was very much hoping she was going to tell again the story about his father's last battle and mysterious disappearance.

"Tell me again why Papa had to go into exile!" he prompted her.

Giving the stew one more quick stir, Ralphie's mother withdrew the large wooden spoon and set it down next to the pot on a little silver plate made expressly for the purpose of setting down stirring spoons to tell a story, leaving it to simmer some more. She then sat down across from him at the round wooden table, as Ralphie waited expectantly for her to begin.

"So, as I've told you many times before, after losing the battle to retain the throne, in which the royal families of the kingdom had been pitted against each other, your father had to go into exile in Languedoc, the kingdom of his great-grandmother's family. Where, rumor has it, he was tracked down ... and murdered ... by your half uncle's assassins." Her voice cracked and broke at the painful memory, and she looked away.

"But we don't know for sure, right, Mama?" Ralphie reminded her, in an effort to comfort her. "He could still be alive, right?" he queried, leaning forward with his questioning, expectant face. "Maybe he could just be in hiding ... and has to be careful for his life?" he put forth, leaning further forward, nodding his head hopefully, wanting her to agree with him.

Looking up, she leaned forward in her chair too, and gave him an intense, searching look before answering. "I don't want you to get your hopes up, Ralphie. The truth is ... we don't know for sure ... and we haven't heard from him in years. But there's been no evidence of his death either. So, in the meantime, his stories help keep him alive in our hearts!"

Upon hearing this confounding answer once again, Ralphie slumped back in his chair, sighing wistfully. "I know. I just wish I could remember what his voice sounded like … I miss him."

"I know you do … so do I, " she consoled. "Nevertheless, fortunately or unfortunately, this is how things stand, and we have to make the best of it! At the moment, it may seem as if providence has dealt us a cruel blow—"

"You mean because he's gone—and may never return?" he interrupted with welling concern.

Hearing the concern in his voice, she gently replied, "Partly … but fortunes and fates can change with time, so we must always keep that in mind! Remember what your uncle Florio was so fond of saying? 'No state of affairs is good or bad, that overthinking makes it so!'"

With this, she flipped the conversation away from their present situation to the future, which she always made clear lay beyond their current circumstance. "Very soon now, Ralphie, you're going to have to take on some of your father's responsibilities … and start walking in his footsteps."

Seeing the uncertainty on his face, she added, "I know his footsteps seem big, but don't worry, I feel it in my bones that you'll grow into them just fine! I sense there's something special about you, just like there was with your father. You, like him, are a natural-born pure-heart, and you just simply can't be otherwise; it would go against your very nature to be anybody but Ralphie!

"So, knowing both of you as I do, I believe you're destined to become a renowned philosopher king, a wellspring of all things ennobling and emboldening, gathered from all the questing you'll do in all the other kingdoms you'll visit. Which, my son, is your calling ... your destiny ... your mission ... to become one of the greatest philosopher kings the world has ever known! Just as it was your father's and his father's before him.

"But for now, it's a secret mission, Ralphie, and so, while you're still in training, you must never, ever, tell anyone!"

"My secret mission!" he gasped. "But can't I at least tell Bucky? He wouldn't tell anyone!"

Bucky was Ralphie's best friend, but Bucky wasn't his real name. His real name was Julian Bartholomew Aloysius Pembroke Willoughby Chatsworth III. But because his two front fangs protruded much like a beaver's buckteeth, and combined with the shortness of his snout, to all his friends he looked more like a beaver than a dragon. So everyone just called him Bucky.

"No, not *anyone*! Especially not Bucky."

"But why?"

"Because Bucky's a blabbermouth. And that could put you, and even him, in dangerous danger! It might even bring about an untimely death for the both of you!"

"But if I had my inheritance," Ralphie objected, "I'd have a retinue, and I'd have guards to protect me, and even Bucky—" He stopped mid-sentence as he thought again about his grandfather's and his own father's fate at the claws of his half uncle and the Bronze Dragons, and the treachery within their retinues that must have taken place. Then, looking down, he saw his underbelly had changed color, and felt a little bit embarrassed—he'd gone pale at her words.

For a Green Dragon going pale meant that his underbelly had turned yellow, and sometimes his knees would knock, or his voice would crack into pops and whistles, which were embarrassing symptoms of death-dread Ralphie had no control over. So he knew he couldn't even have faked his courage if an

assassin were to catch him out in the open, and so had no idea what he'd do when that moment arrived. He was a worrywart about the subject of death, whether his grandfather's, his father's, or his own. And what he was most worried about was whether he would find his courage when his own moment of truth arrived.

Seeing his change in color, his mother's face went soft, and she tried to hearten him. "Even so, I fully believe that your being born without fancy clothes and fancy titles, and not having a lot of fancy bric-a-brac, like golden candelabras and silken tapestries, and servants and such, that your being born into a royal family without a kingdom to call our own was without doubt your most fortunate good fortune!"

"Good fortune?" Ralphie argued. "I don't understand. Why would it be good fortune to be a prince without a kingdom?" thinking nothing could be better than to have a kingdom of his own, and because asking about his father and his family's history had become a game of wits of sorts, wherein she'd test him, and he'd see if he could meet her challenges.

"Because, when you rule a kingdom," she replied, "you often have to deal with bureaucratic bumblers, bullying barons, and backbiting blabbermouths!" Naming just a few of her more favored targets. "But mostly because being a prince without a kingdom lets you see the world without the blinders of high office. That way, as you apprentice as a knight errant to become a proper philosopher king, you can observe how the world really works. And a practical part of that training is learning how to be invisible, and being without royal privilege helps you be invisible. But I know you already know all that!"

"Papa thought being invisible was one of the most important parts of being a proper king, didn't he?" Ralphie asked, prodding her to tell him more about his missing and mystifying, but nonetheless, realer-than-real father, and to ask any questions he may not have thought of during the first hundred tellings.

"Yes … yes he did. And do you remember the three tenets of a pure heart he always practiced to help make himself invisible?"

"I think so. Humility," Ralphie started off confidently. Then, after a thoughtful pause, he added with a beaming smile, "Integrity!" But then, distracted by a frog and a butterfly that appeared to be dancing a duet, he started stammering and stalling. "And … and … aaannnddd …" And then, when he saw the flirty frog murder the beautiful butterfly with his daggerous tongue, his memory suddenly blew a cog! So that ultimately he was unable to remember the remaining tenet, due to the

165

disquieting distraction that had taken place in a corner of the cave, so he just trailed off.

"Yes, humility and integrity, that's right," she nodded as he stalled, lifting him to higher ground with the wings of her words. "And let's not forget sincerity too! These tenets of the Order of the Heart guided your father's path wherever he wandered. And he believed that the most important insights to husbanding a fertile kingdom could only be learned through the careful observation and rough experience of those who are invisible."

By now Ralphie was on the edge of his chair, sitting on his knees, leaning over his dinner bowl, spellbound with her every word, even though he'd heard these stories a hundred times before and knew what was coming. His mother smiled indulgently at him before she stood and returned to the fireplace to check on the simmering stew. He could tell from her smile that she wasn't finished, and he knew that sometimes in her retellings she would show him new ideas, by adding details he'd never heard before, so she had his full attention, now that the butterfly murder was over and almost forgotten.

"Which is exactly why," she went on to explain, "he often traveled alone and incognito when performing his most important princely tasks and duties. He'd oftentimes dress in worker's clothes on these outings, so that he could see what was really going on in the kingdom. One day as a cobbler, another as a fisherman, or on yet another as a merchant of some sort."

"But I still think that going around with your entourage of office would be better!" Ralphie insisted adamantly. "I mean, everybody'd be nice to you, and you'd get the nicest room for the night, and meet the nicest dragons, and eat the best food!" he reasoned, imagining himself going from village to village as an honored guest, visiting friends and relatives, while wearing the finest fitting clothes, and staying at the nicest inns, and eating all the best foods. "And even better—if there ever was trouble—you wouldn't be alone and on your own!"

She briefly turned to glance at him, a look of concern flashing across her face as she did, and it gave him pause. So he asked … or stated … or worried aloud, "I mean, if you're not wearing your regalia of office someone might mistake you for a vagrant or a beggar or a nomad, and maybe make you a serf and press you into bondage! Or even kill you over something foolish, because they'd think you're a just a poor lost soul with no title, no friends, no family—no nothing—and nobody'd ever know where you went off to, or even if you were alive … or dead!"

"I see what you're saying, Ralphie, and it's all true. But your father was willing to take that risk for the good of the kingdom, even though he knew it was fraught with peril! So somehow, in spite of his fear, he'd summon the courage to wander the realm incognito, hiding in plain sight, sometimes even courting death, but always making careful observations and recording what he'd seen and heard, so he could bring back the wisdom he'd learned on his many adventures, and share it in the stories he told."

"But why? Why would he take that chance?" Ralphie wondered aloud confusedly. "How could any story be worth so much risk?"

"Because these weren't just stories that he gathered, Ralphie. They were parables and allegories and myths, full of the wisdom of the many dragons and people he'd met—filled with wild details and larger-than-life characters! Stories that helped keep him and his friends informed and humble in their hearts. So he did it for the benefit of all."

Her stories about his father always made Ralphie dream of his own questing, and his own kingdom to come—a world in which he would someday rule a fertile and just kingdom. Sometimes, the telling of these tales would make her laugh, and other times they would bring memories to her mind that had the power to break her heart anew.

"Tell me again what a great littérateur Papa was!" Ralphie begged. Not to be annoying, or to break her heart, but because her answers made his imagination fly and swell with pride. And for a brief time he could feel, or sense, or even drink-in, his father's martial confidence by way of her stories—stories that were filled with many exploits of derring-do, as well as sentiments of love and pride.

"Oh, Ralphie, the gentle flame of his words always spoke to my heart. He was the purest-hearted dragon I've ever known, and that's why he could write so poetically. That's why I loved him—and still do—for the noble intent of his sentiments. In that way, you're a lot like him. I so wish you could remember him ... but you were so little when he had to leave," she sighed sadly, before telling him once again the story of his father's greatest achievement in bringing to life the tenets of the legendary Order of the Heart.

Ralphie's spirit swelled at this comparison to his father, and his eyes darted to the family shield, hanging on the wall by one of the bookcases near him. The shield was divided into four quarters, each emblazoned with a heraldic emblem. In the first quarter, on a field of gold, was the rampant dragon of his grandfather's family. In the second, was a quill pen lying across an open book, and in the third, a Juniper Tree, both on fields of silver. In its fourth quarter, on a field of green, was emblazoned a heart with a banner across it that read, "Veritas, Pulchritudo, Bonitatem." Which in Latin means "Truth, Beauty, Goodness," the motto of the Order of the Heart.

Seeing the direction of his gaze, she went on to say, "As you know, that shield shows not only the story of our royal lineage, but it also shows the values and aspirations of our family.

"Your father was already a prince by birth, and a knight by training, and as first-born, he would've been king by birthright, of course. Except he wasn't an ordinary Green Dragon, he was a philosopher by calling. He often told me that even as a child he'd wondered what his purpose was in the world … and who'd made the world … and how far it was to the stars … and what lay beyond.

"So he was apprenticing, not just to be a regular king, mind you, but to be a philosopher king, which involves a lot of writing. And I see so much of him in you that I know it's your calling too. That's why your philosophical apprenticeship is so important. That's why the writing's so important."

"Ohhhh … but writing's so *hard*!" Ralphie lamented, laboring out a heavy sigh as he rolled his eyes to the ceiling. "I never know where to start … besides, I feel like everything

I do write is *boring* ... I'd rather eat worms than write! Can't I become a philosopher king some other way?"

"Eat worms? Really? But no, there is no other way. Your father was becoming a philosopher king by *way* of his writing, and the more he wrote the better he got at refining his thoughts, which also made him a great orator. Kings have to be good speechifiers too, you know. Because, as I've told you so many times before, being a king is not all about swashbuckling! Your father got so good at speechifying that I encouraged him to publish his speeches, so he wouldn't be away from home so much.

"He'd openly write about justice for all, and natural rights, and against serfdom—and his pen soon became sharper than his sword! He wanted to put an end to feudalism, a stance that the barons found very threatening, because he'd dared give voice to the voiceless. But the invisible people, the forgotten people, the hurt, the dispossessed, the common people, loved him for it!

"It was your father's belief that everyone was born equal, with inherent natural rights. Thus, it was his emboldening and ennobling ideas of individual sovereignty that eventually forced him onto that particular battlefield in the Great War on Ignorance. He realized that if there was to be a fertile kingdom after your grandfather's death, that it was his destiny, in service to the Holy Grail, to take up that fight." A look of profound heart sorrow crossed her face at those words, and she paused, lowering her gaze, and Ralphie could see she was once again lost in disquieting thoughts.

"Don't be sad, Mama," Ralphie comforted softly, his voice turning into a blue-white flame that seemed to envelop her in love.

She looked at him tenderly; unshed tears caught in her lashes, seeing her husband's pure heart reflected in Ralphie's concern. Then, collecting herself, she ladled the stew into bowls and brought them to the table, as she resolutely continued to guide him. He was, after all, their legacy to the world. "Your father wrote about what he felt in his heart in his journal. He was the Marcus Aurelius of his time!" she declared, her eyes glowing with pride, as a soft smile illuminated her face.

Tucking his napkin into his scales, Ralphie asked, between slurping spoonfuls of stew, "Marcus who?"

"Marcus Aurelius. He was a great Roman Emperor. He ruled Rome for twenty years without scandal or corruption! And when he died, he left behind his personal journal, which he asked a close friend to burn upon his death. The friend read it, but instead of burning it, published it. Because, he reasoned, the wisdom it contained would help bring light into the world.

"Your father kept several journals. When he was away on a secret mission, he'd always start with a fresh one, which he would log with his other field journals, upon his return.

"He also kept a secret journal, which he'd let me read. In it were some of the most beautiful words I'd ever read! Healing words, inspiring words, ennobling words—words that could bring confused, strife-ridden, hurt souls together. In it he wrote down his more revolutionary ideas regarding the building of a fertile kingdom, a kingdom in which everyone had a voice," she went on to say, placing a basket of warm biscuits and a small porcelain butter dish on the table, before sitting down again to join him.

"I never had the chance to read all of it, but he assured me in his excitement, on many occasions, that he'd discerned how your half uncle, his court minions, and the Bronze Dragons, could be subdued without violence … he was hoping to win them over to his ideas with his speeches, plays, and poetry!"

"Really? He did? What happened to it?" Ralphie wanted to know, buttering a biscuit before stuffing it into his mouth.

"It was lost when they seized our lands—or so your half uncle claimed," she answered, a cautious skepticism woven into her words. "But I never believed him, because from time-to-time I've heard your father's words repeated in some of the villages I've visited.

"At any rate, at one time our family was considered untouchable … and when your grandfather was alive, the kingdom *was* fertile, and the people were happy, and your father never considered his secret journal would become the reason for the war!

"But shortly after your grandfather's sudden death, your half uncle claimed the throne, and put a bounty on your father! Our own lands were confiscated shortly thereafter, and we, along with the families of our supporters, were forced into exile. Some were even sold into slavery by the Bronze Dragons! And, as you know, the kingdom has since become a wasteland."

Bronze Dragons were everywhere now, all along the borders of the enchanted forest where Ralphie and his mother lived in exile. Ever since he could remember, he'd heard innumerable stories recounting their erratic cruelty and capricious violence, in countless infamous tragedies of how they'd turned once fertile kingdoms into smoldering wastelands.

Legend had it that they were responsible for the cruelest mayhem and most violent chaos in the Land of the Clock-Watchers. Mercenaries in their greed, guileless in their lying, to this day their favorite cruelty is to make their victims betray themselves, or their subjects, by seducing them with their own vanities, and then mocking them for having fallen prey to their banal blandishments and devious deceptions.

"In fact," his mother went on to tell him, "rumor had it that many years ago, in the great battles for the trade routes of the Sea of Marmara, they held untold numbers of port cities hostage, and ransomed the Caliphate of Umayyad for their liberation! It's said that they'd capture the town's populace, including Green Dragons, auctioning the people off in the slave markets of Acre and Alexandria. But the Green Dragons ... the Green Dragons they killed torturously. Drawing and quartering them in public spectacles, then selling their body parts as talismans to witchdoctors and greedy politicians, and mostly, the clergy—who paid the highest price!"

Ralphie gulped, and then sneezed hard. Except it wasn't really a sneeze, it was a flameout, a flame that had choked itself out as it left his throat. So all that came out were a just few puffs of smoke, followed by a loud pop that turned itself into a fizzling hiss before finally becoming a sputtering series of snorts and whistles. Which was embarrassing, even if his mother was the only one who'd heard or seen this awkward display of a very well founded fear.

"I know you fear the Bronze Dragons, Ralphie—and rightly so!" she said gently. "Your father was wary of them too. But I know from all the talks your father and I shared that he believed he'd found a way to defeat them. That's why I'm teaching you your father's vision of a kingdom that doesn't need to use violence or cruelty to enforce its tenets—a kingdom with its foundation built on the Chivalric Code—a philosophical kingdom."

"But how would I do that? Create a kingdom like that?"

"It's gong to take a lot of hard work, Ralphie!" she sighed heavily. "For the kingdom to become fertile once again, you must first learn how to be a thoughtful and just ruler ... one who's willing to do the humbling hard work it takes to become a philosopher, before anything else! Otherwise, you'd be little different than your half uncle, who's driven by greed and power, more than by grace and wisdom.

"One day soon, when you're ready, when your schooling's done, and you've educated yourself to your own satisfaction, it'll be time for you to follow in your father's footsteps and explore incognito, not only our lands, but also all the other lands that your questing takes you to in your search for the Grail. In this way, just like him, you'll learn the ways of a variety of kingdoms, both big and small, and thus become worldly-wise from your peripatetic wanderings ... from questing, Ralphie, from questing."

She'd mentioned this before, the need to become worldly-wise, but Ralphie had forgotten to look it up in his dictionary, so he just looked at her uncomprehendingly at first.

"Don't you see? That's why you have to become a philosopher first, so you can reflect wisely ... and thus be able to rule justly when the time comes! So right now there are larger challenges you must undertake, to ennoble and embolden yourself, for the days *after* the defining battle of your life."

But then he immediately put forth, as he always did, what he thought was the most obvious, simplest, magnificent, dramatic, spectacular, fantastic, brilliant solution to their situation. "But since it rightfully belonged to us ... why don't we just raise our own army ... and overthrow the usurpers and reclaim it?" he wondered aloud, as if he hadn't heard any of her instruction on the importance of the non-violent aspects of being a wise and just ruler. Imagining instead, sword fights on crenulated fortress walls, and swinging from tapestries and chandeliers in all the grand halls of the land, out-swashbuckling every foe with a distinctive double slash of his sword—and putting forth boldly, "We could conquer the usurpers with our army and derring-do alone! Just like Alexandre the Great did!"

"Oh, Ralphie, it won't be that simple. How I wish it was! Although no one would ever deny us the right to win our lands back with violence ... but where would that lead us? Just to more violence, and violence only breeds more fear. You *could* slash and stab your way to the top, Ralphie, but everyone would be afraid of you and not respect you, and no one would ever want to get close to you and be a true friend. And you'd have to keep stabbing and slashing just to stay on top. You couldn't trust anyone, and so you'd have to rule alone—just like your half uncle! All wise and just kings know that trust and good faith are the very currency of a fertile kingdom.

"So, as I always keep telling you, it's not all about the swashbuckling derring-do! Before our kingdom can be restored, before you can ascend to the throne, there's much for you to learn and do!" Seeing the unfocused, faraway look in his eyes, she stopped mid-thought. "Ralphie, are you listening?"

"Huh? What?" Still lost in swashbuckling imaginings, Ralphie could only give her his startled questioning face for the umpteenth time and then shrug his shoulders, his favorite combination of a half dozen expressions that he had in his repertoire for whenever he didn't have the words for being taken by surprise, or was confused, or felt exasperated because his imaginings had been interrupted.

To recapture his attention, she conceded his earlier point about raising an army and going to battle to reclaim the throne. "I know I've told you many times before that it's not all about derring-do. But it's also fair to say that violence—in the defense of the good—is at times unavoidable!"

Ralphie sat up stiffly when she said those words, because she rarely spoke of the just use of violence. She was a peace lover.

"The truth is, sometimes we *have* to fight for what we believe in! So I want you to be ready for that moment of truth too, for when you come face-to-face with the usurpers in a do-or-die battle for the throne … like your father had to … maybe even unto …" She didn't want to speak of death, so her words turned into a yielding refrain at those fate-filled thoughts, and a shudder seemed to go up her ridge scales. But then, perhaps out of not wanting him to catch scent of her fear for him, she put on her brave face as she returned to the table and ladled more stew into his bowl.

Ralphie had been holding his breath unconsciously during her speechifying on violence, pondering the depths of do-or-die situations with his half uncle and his Bronze Dragon minions, and he started to turn pale again.

Then, because she knew her son, and knew how to spark his imagination whenever the mention of death cooled his enthusiasm for proper knight errantry training, she went on to add, while filling her own bowl, "In the meantime, there's always the rewarding work of saving distressed damsels imprisoned in tall towers … and slaying the monsters that keep them captive, and the accolades and booty that go with such work. And yes, that may even mean fighting brutish Bronze Dragons! Who I say are nothing more than bullies who've been bullied! Some of whom might only be in need of a good hug to see the error of their ways."

Smiling crazily at the notions of violence in the service of the good, along with huggable foes, Ralphie went back to his daydream fantasies of heroic swashbuckling derring-do on castle walls and in grand halls. This time slaying with ease the brutish Bronze Dragons that dared fight him, knowing they were little more than bullies in need of a good hug. Therefore, those that submitted to his hugs, he instructed in the ways of the Code, thereby relieving them of their brutishness. And for those that didn't submit, by using his famous double slash swordplay!

Seeing his eyes glaze over once again, she despaired of ever getting through to him. "Oh, Ralphie, are you hearing *anything* I'm saying?" she gently rebuffed him for the umpteenth time, just as his imagination was about to leave the station.

"Huh? What?" Ralphie replied, giving her his questioning face with a shoulder shrug again, having been interrupted just as he was about to board a thought train to who knows where.

Shaking her head, his mother continued patiently, "To do that properly, you need to go to school every day, and quit playing hooky with Bucky—honestly, Ralphie, I never know where you are except when it's time to eat—and, and," and then, spying a pile of scattered schoolbooks just inside the entry, she went on to add, "and get your things out of the hallway ... and clean your room, it's a mess!" going on to address a million other seemingly mundane duties associated with the colossal enterprise of becoming a proper philosopher prince like his father.

At about the same time that Ralphie and his mother embarked on their theatrical adventures into their own world of chivalric heroics at the evening supper table, she also began to encourage him to start journaling. Which, of course, he immediately found inconsistent with his ideas of princely duties and responsibilities that mostly revolved around courtly costumes and ceremonial ceremonies, when not engaged in swashbuckling derring-do.

"But I told you ... I'm no good at it! And besides, my life's so *boring* ... nothing exciting *ever* happens!"

"Well, Ralphie, if your life's so boring, then why don't you write about our imaginary adventures? And maybe include your friends, and Loudmouth too, if you can."

Ralphie had never considered this idea before, as simple and obvious as it was. Because for some odd reason, and no one had told him so, he felt that journaling was strictly a place to record what had happened to him in his daily life. The thought that imaginal adventuring was actually "allowed" in journaling ... and that journaling could be a form of questing ... had never occurred to him. And when he did realize it, the old boring world of journaling became a new theatre for his imagination.

In light of his mother's suggestion, journaling soon took on a realer-than-real life of its own, as his imagination gave him inestimable inspirations at the drop of a hat, the bark of a dog, or the discovery of a peculiarly magical word, spinning forth new heroic narratives, wherein he was always the leading character who would save the world with a vigorous enthusiasm—an élan vital—like Alexandre the Great!

He soon became so inventive in his narratives that just to keep up with him, his mother took to scrapbooking his outlandish tales with her own illustrations, and made both of them homemade regalia. Which for him included some of his father's medals, as well as medallions on sashes, and a wooden sword, and for both of them magnificent hats, all so they could travel together in style, in his elaborately extravagant imaginings.

Not only was this playacting spurred on by Ralphie's wondrous wonderings, along with the stories his mother told of their family history, but also by their reading of the legend of King Arthur and the quest for the Holy Grail, as well as the various other adventures of the Knights of the Round Table. His mother further encouraged this outlandish play by plying him with books about Renaissance history.

Thus inspired, Ralphie had soon re-made their world, their nightly supper world, into a theatrically imaginal world of knights and lords and chevaleresses and ladies of the court, acting out all kinds of intrigue and various machinations concerning overthrowing usurpers, and dealing with kingly rights and princely duties. All duly recorded in his unbelievably fantabulous, far-fetched, yet incredibly plausible, probable, and even possible, journalings.

In addition to all that, to keep him busy when she didn't have time to answer his millions and millions of questions, especially the ones she didn't have answers to, she had him memorize the

proper names and duties of various court functionaries, along with their proper costumes, and so on and so forth.

But as different challenges of running a kingdom would be put to him by his mother, a bookish knowledge would take hold of him, leading him to enthusiastically recite, like an overflowing fountain, all the courtly ceremonial nuances and their historical significance, including the reasons for their pertaining codes of conduct. This, along with his intoxication with King Arthur and the trials and tribulations of his knights and the stories of the troubadours, gave rise in him a need to show-off this bookish knowledge, which resulted in his constantly blurting out non sequitur, know-it-all quips, without the slightest provocation.

"Did you know there's a special person at court who arranges all the royal journeys? He's called the Clerk of the Green Cloth! And there's a Keeper of the Swans, too. I think that'd be a great job, cause I could fly with the swans every day! Except in winter, then I'd want to be the Keeper of Ice and Snow—he collects the snow, you know, and makes it into ice for the royal court's sherbets!"

"And let's not forget there's also a royal librarian too, Ralphie," she reminded him. "For me, that would be the best job I could ever imagine! When I was your age, I spent almost all my spare time, like you, reading, lost in books. That's how I did all my traveling and adventuring, back when I was your age," she with a wistful, faraway look.

"Yes, but if I could have any job at court, I think I'd like to be the Master of the Robes! He gets to stage all the courtly costumes for the king. Or maybe I could be the Keeper of the Regalia, because he gets to take care of all the king's accoutrements of office!"

But then his mind turned to the Master of the Revels, which he also wanted to be. The Master of the Revels was a position that was responsible for organizing all the royal festivities, and for entertaining the king by way of private plays, that the king alone reviewed. In that capacity he served as court jester, the only one allowed to make jokes about anything or anyone, including the king, in his plays, and not get banished from court!

Then Ralphie's mind turned to the Groom Extraordinary of the Chamber. Which might be an even better choice, he thought, because he had a secretive and mysterious role, as both a regular actor in the Company of the King's Men, as a cover, and also, whenever the king's bragging had gotten out of control, in protecting the king's reputation from spurious aspersions, which was his real role—usually accomplished through droll wit, or silly jest, or nonsensical speechifying. And, even better, when his wordplay didn't work, as a last resort he could legally turn to swordplay, under the protection of the king himself.

Then, in the midst of all these listings, Ralphie suddenly began to laugh, almost falling out of his chair, as he blurted out breathlessly, "Did you know there's a special person at court who wipes the king's bottom? He's called the Groom of the Stool!"

"I do know that!" his mother chuckled. "It's actually a very sought-after, and much respected position! Except that nobody ever wanted to shake his hand. So to avoid it, people started bowing. Pretty soon, everybody was bowing to everybody else whenever they didn't want to shake someone's hand, for lots of other reasons, until the whole thing got out of control! But that's another story."

Still laughing, she asked, "And did you know there's also a special person at court who kills the rats? He's called the Royal Rat-Killer," playfully punctuating her words with a shiver and a little mousey squeal.

"I think their uniform's the best! Did you know it's got rats embroidered all over it?" he shared excitedly, his eyes getting dreamy as he imagined himself proudly wearing the uniform of the Royal Rat-Killer to various social functions.

"Their uniforms *are* quite resplendent, I do agree! I've always loved royal courts ... there're so many wonderful roles to play ... it's a great, beautiful theatre! But you know, I think the most challenging role on that stage is to be the queen of the philosopher king!" she winked knowingly. "Now, tell me more about how a young, princely knight errant demonstrates chivalry."

Needing no further encouragement, Ralphie happily continued to show-off with his non-sequitur declarations. "A knight errant must fight for the welfare of all!" he stated emphatically, smashing fist his on the table. "And have nothing to do with meanness or deceit either! And he must never betray a confidence, and always be faithful to his promises—no matter how big or small. And a knight errant must be loyal to his country and his fellow knights too! And he must always be hospitable and gracious, and put the needs of others before his own! And he must always do what's right, even if no one's watching! And if a knight breaks his oath, he could be stripped of his titles and lands!" he rattled off proudly, barely stopping to take a breath.

"True ... all true, but I remind you once again, you don't want to sound like a know-it-all bookworm. And you don't want ask too many questions either." Then, finally having given up on all other approaches to get him to quiet down, she told him, "If you show your ignorance by being annoying, you're sure to get taken for a fool by a usurper!"

Untroubled by her challenging words about being an annoying know-it-all, Ralphie slurped up his last few spoonfuls of stew, licked the bowl clean, then continued reciting in dribs and drabs the parts of the Code that worked to give his fantastical imaginings flare.

"And a knight errant must always be brave and have courage in all kinds of fearful situations! That's why it's called derring-do!" he claimed. Then, slamming his paw on the table again, he further declared, "And he must never ever avoid a dangerous but true path out of fear!"

"Except, as I've told you a million times before, it's *not* all about derring-do!" she sighed and scolded for the umpteenth time. "I mean ... how can you serve the less fortunate if you die in a sword fight? Need I remind you, a knight errant is also committed to defending the weak and poor and helpless, too! And so, I put it to you again—how are you going to do any of that if you end up dead?" shooting him a stern look as she cleared the dinner bowls and went to the flat skillet on the firebox, to whip up their favorite dessert of pancakes with elderberry syrup.

"I know, I know ... but don't worry, Mama! I won't die in a swordfight. Of all my friends I'm the best swordfighter! So the only way anybody'd ever get me is by trickery—and they could only take me prisoner if I didn't have a sword! And, if I *were* taken prisoner, I'd give up my horse—and pledge to never fight that opponent ever again!"

"But dragons don't have horses, Ralphie!"

Ever ready for her challenges, he replied confidently, "But I do! Loudmouth. He's my horse!" Loudmouth was his mutt dog, which he'd named Loudmouth because of his incessant barking.

"Well, alright, I could see that, I suppose. So Loudmouth is your horse. But why does the Code say to never fight that opponent ever again? Why would that be, Ralphie?"

"Because ... by not killing you ... he ... he showed you mercy?" he both declared and asked at the same time.

"Exactly! And mercy is superior to violence because ... ?" She let her words trail off, and looked at Ralphie expectantly.

Now stymied because they hadn't gone over that part of the lesson on mercy for some time, Ralphie tried his best anyway.

"Because … because you could be wrong. And you wouldn't want to hurt somebody who's innocent … out of ignorance."

"Excellent! It seems to me your training's coming along just fine," she told him encouragingly. "And remember, the truly noble love mercy … and delight in saving men's souls above all else. You know, your father believed that the practice of mercy is the real evidence of nobility."

"I know, I remember."

Recharged by her praise, he started squirming in his chair again, eager to continue showing off his knowledge of all things about the court, codes, and questing, and absentmindedly started to reel off chivalric facts that sometimes ran smack into chivalric fates.

"And a knight errant must never ever gang up on an opponent! He must only fight one-on-one!" Ralphie went on to tell her. "And he must always defend defenseless damsels in imminent danger … unto … unto death!" At this, his voice cracked unexpectedly, and a pop and a whistle came out, and so he gulped hard, as a look of woe and worry flashed across his face, as it always did on the parts of the Code dealing with death oaths.

Ralphie had worked out the notion of death in two ways. There was death-death, where you actually, physically died. Then there was being pushed through death's door, where you died of public mortification, which was as close to death as anyone would ever want to get, but were still alive.

So that when he blurted out his own tenet, which wasn't part of the Code, "That's why you should never turn your back on a foe. Cause he could push you through death's door and into real death—and you might never return!" it made sense ... to him.

Since Ralphie had been pushed through death's door more than once, and had had to make his way back from these multiple mortifying mortifications, when it came to death and dying, he knew by these experiences that some deaths were sufferable. But when he thought about real physical death, where you couldn't make a come back, like maybe his father couldn't come back, he always gulped hard, he couldn't help it.

At these thoughts of death and dying, Ralphie paused. But only long enough to take a few more forkfuls of pancakes before flaring up again, brightening as he remembered the last part of the Code that dealt with returning philosopher kings.

Grabbing his goblet of orange juice, he held it aloft with both paws, as if it were the Grail itself, and swore an oath of fidelity to the Order of the Heart, and then drank from it ceremoniously, the way the ritual was described in the story of Sir Galahad. Caught up in the momentum of the moment, he then went on waving his fork madly as he continued to speechify crazily about the Code, and King Arthur, and proper questing.

"And when you return from all your questing, you must share with your people the wisdom you've gathered on your adventures in seeking the Grail, by way of the tales you tell in the stories you share!" he exclaimed proudly, punctuating his final words by stabbing a peach with his fork, and presenting it as an orb of office to his mother, while holding a large serving spoon in his other paw as if it were a royal scepter.

Taking the peach orb and spoon scepter he offered her with royal deference, his mother smiled, and the warmth of her ethereal spirit filled him with pride, making them both glow, literally glow. Because they were Green Dragons after all, and when Green Dragons are filled with confidence and dignity and gratefulness and delight in themselves, they glow a soft blue on their bellies. This happens when they believe, truly believe, the sentiments of their words, which emit a warm blue glow as they speak them aloud, that comes out as a soothing blue flame.

After which, because parents know that you can't just play the day away, his mother placed the serving spoon scepter in the empty serving bowl. She then hesitated for a moment before clearing the rest of the table, and reminded him, "I know you know this, Ralphie, but in case you've forgotten, Alexandre the Great's tutor was one of the most famous philosophers of all time—Aristotle! Now please, hand me that fork before you poke yourself in the eye!"

If you've enjoyed this book, and we hope you did,
please post a review on Amazon.
It's the best way for independent authors like us
to gain exposure and help sales.

Thank you!

Made in the USA
Monee, IL
31 October 2024

68414203R00121